M.T. CONNOR

Thorns of Love

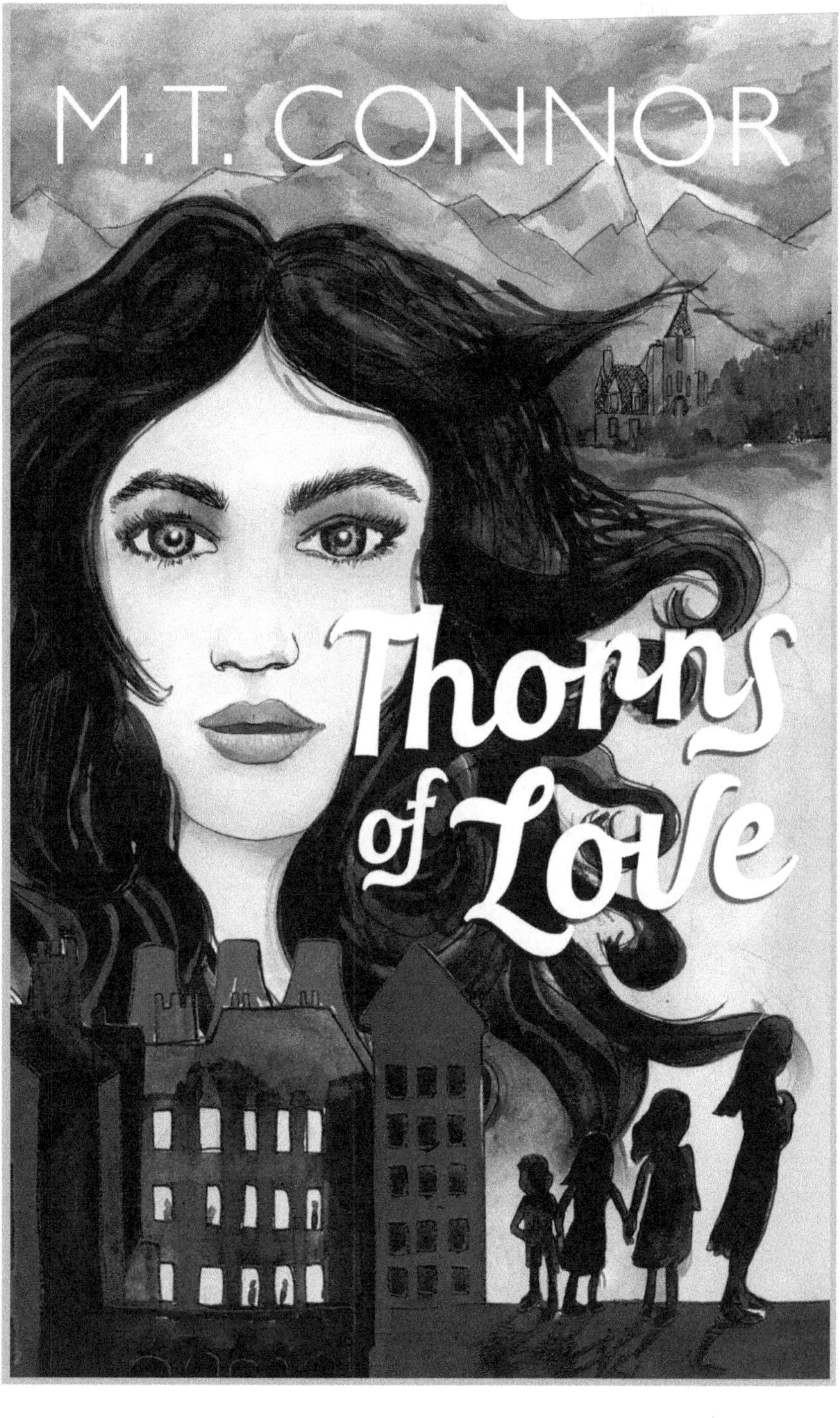

Thorns of Love

by

M T Connor

Copyright M.T.Connor 2012

ISBN: 978-0-9546564-1-6

Formatting for the Kindle and epub version - KindleMonster.com

Table of Contents

Chapter One..1
Chapter Two...6
Chapter Three...7
Chapter Four..9
Chapter Five...12
Chapter Six..18
Chapter Seven..23
Chapter Eight..28
Chapter Nine...31
Chapter Ten..37
Chapter Eleven...40
Chapter Twelve...44
Chapter Thirteen...49
Chapter Fourteen...59
Chapter Fifteen..63
Chapter Sixteen..71
Chapter Seventeen..76
Chapter Eighteen...86
Chapter Nineteen...96
Chapter Twenty...99
Chapter Twenty One..110
Chapter Twenty Two..119
Chapter Twenty Three..124
Chapter Twenty Four...132
Chapter Twenty Five...137
Chapter Twenty Six..143
Chapter Twenty Seven..145
Chapter Twenty Eight..147
Chapter Twenty Nine...149
Chapter Thirty..152
Chapter Thirty One..160
Chapter Thirty Two..165
Chapter Thirty Three..172
Chapter Thirty Four...177

Chapter Thirty Five..180
Chapter Thirty Six...189
Chapter Thirty Seven...195
Chapter Thirty Eight..199
Chapter Thirty Nine...202
Chapter Forty...208

About the Author

Mary T. Connor was born 1947 was raised in Salford, Lancashire, England. Married with five children and ten grandchildren, she still lives in Salford.

Dedication

I would like to say thank you to my family for their patience and understanding. To Peter my husband and children Danny, Francis and Stephen (particularly for his criticism) Elizabeth and Peter, to Claire Maxwell, Claire Connor, Sister Sue, Andrea and Aunt Jesse. To Ava and `The Kersal Writers Group' Lynda Maude for her support and expertise, to Ian Hobson for his patience and finally a special thank you to Steve Giller for giving me the confidence to write, without which this story would never have been told.

Chapter One.

It was a perfect summer evening; the sky was a clear blue as the sun made its way down towards the snowy peaks of the distant mountains. It was warm and dry with just a hint of a breeze. People seemed to float around in the most exquisite and colourful clothes that Ailsa had only ever seen in magazines. It was a wonderful party, and it was hers.

"Happy darling?"

"Oh yes Ma, I have never been so happy in all my life"

Fiona Fleming smiled as she watched her daughter's radiant face. Was she sixteen already? How time had passed.

Ailsa felt overwhelmed by all the happiness inside her. But then quite suddenly she felt as though she was being watched. She couldn't help herself, curiosity got the better of her. Quietly she left the party and made her way down towards the trees. Someone was there, she could feel it.

"You are like something straight from the Gods above" whispered a voice so soft she couldn't be sure if it was real or not.

But there, emerging slowly from amongst the trees, was the shadow of a man. The most handsome man she had ever seen. In the dimness of the descending light, Ailsa could only guess at the darkness of his eyes, but his hair was wild and black. He smiled, a strong wide smile that captivated her imagination and her heart.

Was it the one glass of wine, or the feeling of a dreamlike unreality, but whatever it was, she didn't resist when he took her into his arms and danced under the moonlight. And when he kissed her she was filled with a wonderful new emotion.

She could feel his warm breath upon her face as his lips gently brushed past hers, the smell of earthy strength gave him a mysterious aura as he held her close. Her breathing became rapid as she clung to him. Then, as if it was the most natural thing in the world, he quietly and slowly aroused a passion she never knew existed. All sense of reality became lost. And there under the shadow of darkness he took her. Two bodies joined as one, each wrapped in the others embrace as the quietness of night enveloped them in the sweetness of love. It was there, as she lay in his arms smiling and contented in a dreamlike world, that her father found them.

The fury of his voice filled the night. He could be heard far and wide as he screamed abuse at her, and the common beast that had had the audacity to accost his daughter and to bring the worst possible shame, to the family name. But more painful than that was the fact he had dishonoured the most precious thing in his life, Ailsa. Taking her arm, he dragged her back to the house threatening the man who now looked like he was trying to make a quick escape. In all his life he hadn't felt such pain or endured so great an embarrassment. His guests had left, his wife had retired to her rooms in a flood of tears, and before him was the monster who had caused it. He was devastated. He had no choice. There would have to be a wedding.

The following weeks amid tears and the inability to understand anything anymore, Ailsa was heartbroken. Apparently she had committed the unforgivable sin, sex before marriage with a foreigner. Nobody seemed to love her any more, and she didn't know why. Her mother wouldn't talk to her and her father just kept repeating again and again how he had disowned her.

"What have I done that is so terribly wrong?" she wailed.

But no one listened or answered.

Only Alice the cook would shake her head in despair and say. "You might have a bairn Ailsa,"

"But you only have babies when you are married," She answered, not understanding.

Alice cried all the more.

"How can being rich make you so hard? She's nothing but a bairn and doesn't deserve this. There is no way," Alice thought, "not in a million years is she going to survive out there with him"

The wedding Anton so happily agreed to, proved to be one of the biggest mistakes he had ever made. Instead of welcoming him into the family, they disowned their daughter. Anton learnt too late, the Highlanders of Scotland were very clannish and he was not welcome. They didn't believe in mixed marriages and looked down on him. But the idea of a child of mixed blood being born out of wedlock was unacceptable. That was why they did the honourable thing, gave them a wedding, a small dowry and told them never to return.

As Ailsa left the comfort zone of her homeland, she cried. But then she felt excited, the thought of belonging to Anton was overwhelming. To be able to feel his arms around her, to feel his lips on hers, his touch and soft caresses made her almost faint with pleasure. Since the night her father had found them together, she hadn't been allowed to see him.

"You will wait like any other decent young woman, until you're married", her father had said bitterly.

Anton was everything she had imagined, she loved him with all her heart and when she realised she was pregnant she couldn't have been happier. But it was a sickly pregnancy, long and painful, and Anton wouldn't stop long enough in one place for her to see a doctor. He declared it was the most natural thing in the world and they didn't need anyone. With the small dowry gone, and no more to look forward to, he seemed to change overnight. Gone was the caring loving husband. He became insensitive to her needs. He left her for long periods, sometimes it was for days, and Ailsa had no one to ask what it was like to have a baby, or how long it took. She cried like she had never cried before. She wanted her mother, she needed her, she was frightened and didn't know what to do. Then Anton would appear and carry on as if he had never been away.

The war was on and though she hadn't been aware of anything different at home, she now saw the full impact of pain and poverty. Travelling on the road visiting various towns, putting up with her husband's idleness and adultery, something she desperately wanted to close her eyes to, as the thought of it just broke her heart. But she couldn't, Anton flaunted it in her face, condemning her for tricking him into a marriage he didn't want, sometimes bringing the women out to where they had camped for the night. He laughed at her tears, telling her it was time she grew up. Though Ailsa hated the women he brought, hated hearing them laughing and drinking and having sex, it at least gave her a rest, knowing he would not come to her for his pleasure. But on this particular night, a night where for the first time they stayed on the edge of a small gathering of other Gypsy caravans. She lay there, glad it had at last gone quiet when she realised she couldn't move for the pain, it had been gnawing away at her all day and she didn't know why or what to do. Then her body seemed to take over her mind and she screamed in agony as a vicious pain ripped right through her.

Ailsa remembered only that someone was helping her, a woman. Voices were filtering through, though she was barely conscious, she smiled as she thought she heard someone screaming abuse at Anton. And then it was all over, a child had been born. Exhausted, Ailsa sank into a deep sleep. The sleep seemed endless, like a nightmare that refused to go away. Voices reached out to her, she heard crying, women wailing in the distance and the sound of the wagon as it bounced over the uneven ground.

"Why are we going?" she asked "what is happening?" She didn't know what was real and what wasn't anymore. She just knew the pain and exhaustion that had wrapped itself around her body was unbearable. She had to have some sleep.

"Come on, the bairn needs feeding."

She could hear his words; feel the arms she once loved pulling her up from the makeshift bed, forcing her, making her hold the child. It was a girl, hair as black as his and eyes just as deep and dark. She stared at it.

"She will be called Maria, Maria Rose" Anton stated.

Ailsa didn't care what it was called. She thought of her father.

"You said this would happen. But I didn't believe you. I didn't know how to make babies. No-one told me."

Then she became quiet as she remembered how Anton had laughed at her when she told him, and called her stupid. She had hated him so much at that moment and now as she looked down at the child she realised there was a coldness inside her. It didn't feel like it was hers. There was nothing there, no love, nothing. Overcome with sadness, she put the child down, turned her back, and left the new born infant to cry.

Chapter Two.

"Why do I do it?" Anton muttered to himself as the pain increased with the movement of his body. He knew he had had too much to drink, he always did. But this time it was different. This time he had been wracked with demons and nightmares that had plagued him for most of the night. Somewhere in the back of his mind there was something that wouldn't go away. He had hurt Ailsa, he felt it deep inside, but the need to blame someone had made him lose control. He had done something but couldn't remember what. He had lashed out at them, hurt them. He had been too drunk. Images of his wife flashed before him, she was crying. "But that doesn't really mean anything;" he thought "she is always crying."

Maria was his eldest and had always made him feel uneasy. Something in the back of his mind made him think she had been awake, and somehow involved in what had happened but he couldn't be sure. His second born, John had been asleep along with Cathy the youngest.

Suddenly he shivered and felt cold. An overwhelming feeling of fear seemed to have enveloped him. Flashes of fire and devils, of Maria and witchcraft, heat, pain and the heart rendering cries of his wife suddenly became real. He could feel the screams inside his head getting louder and louder.

"I have to get away, I have to," his body shook and his head ached, the memories pounded away inside. The memories of the night when Maria had been born, he was overcome with fear. He had to get away, to escape. And so as the dawn broke and the rain gently washed over the grass, Anton left.

Chapter Three.

Every day Ailsa waited, she knew she couldn't look after herself let alone the children and so she had done the only thing she could. She had written to her father, begging him to let them come home. But everyday her heart sank deeper and deeper as no word came. She could no longer eat or sleep and then, just as she was about to give up all hope, it came. Clutching it to her chest she could feel her heart pounding as she realised how frightened she was of opening it.

The children gathered around. They could feel the tension in the air; see her trembling as her fingers fumbled with the envelope. She couldn't help it. It had at long last arrived. Slowly and quietly she started to read, her voice low and unsteady. And then quite suddenly she stopped. Her face paled, and her eyes became enlarged as though she was experiencing extreme terror. A large heart rendering cry escaped from somewhere deep inside her as she slumped to the floor.

Maria's heart felt as if it had been ripped open. Her mother was like a sad broken doll, dejected, sitting on the floor with tears that just cascaded down from her face. She looked as if the world had suddenly gone and she was no longer part of anything. Maria knew something terrible had happened and whatever it was, it was there in that letter that now lay discarded on the floor. Slowly she reached out her hand as she quietly bent down and picked it up, and just as silently placed it into her pocket until she could slip away and read it later

The letter was from her grandparents, the very wealthy grandparents her Ma had talked about all her life.

"It will be so wonderful when we are home," she would smile. "Everything will be perfect, we will never be hungry ever again and there are lots of big warm soft beds to lie in. Life will be so good and we shall be so happy."

Her Ma had always said how wonderful her parents were and how, when they all went home, everything would be fine and they would be happy. And they would never know hunger. Except they weren't going home, the letter said so. It said they weren't wanted and not to return.

Maria dropped the letter in a furious temper and stood viciously grinding it into the ground. "How dare they," she screamed "How dare they! Who do they think they are? Who gave them the right to hurt our Ma? It's not fair, it's just not fair."

Once her temper had cooled Maria quietened down, she thought long and hard as to what they could do. She couldn't think of anything, but one thing she was sure about was that although she had never met them, her grandparents were in every aspect worse than her own father. At least he never professed to love then. Between her feelings for her father and now those for her grandparents her whole body shook with rage, and a feeling of pure unadulterated hate.

Meanwhile Ailsa slept, her mind refusing to comprehend anything anymore. Sinister and evil thoughts were all jumbled up inside her. She couldn't remember anything properly except pain and Anton. The only thing that had kept her going was the prospect of going home. And now that too had been snatched away, but somewhere deep inside, her reasoning became confused.

"If it's only Maria who looks like her father," she thought. "then it's only Maria who could be his child." This thought pleased her. "John and Cathy are mine, they look like me, and they look like my father" she smiled. "Yes, he will want us, he will love us," and as her mind took on this strange new idea, it made her happy, it gave her hope. "Maria doesn't belong with us, she belongs to him. It's all her fault, that's why nobody loves me." And with that thought she closed her eyes and sank into a deep sad sleepy world of unreality, from which she never really came out of.

Chapter Four.

Maria had lain there quietly, listening. At first she thought she had dreamt it all, her mother crying, the discarded letter. Then reality hit her, it had all been true, but deep inside, she didn't care anymore. They weren't wanted. It said so in the letter. So why should she want them?

Slowly and quietly she left her makeshift bed on the floor and went in search of food at the first light of dawn. Meanwhile, Ailsa awoke and started sobbing uncontrollably, pulling the blanket tightly around herself. Beside her, trying to share the blanket, were John and Cathy. John was seven years old now and normally a quiet child, but today he was like his sister, cold and hungry. Cathy, three years younger, whimpered incessantly. At eleven years old Maria was at breaking point. She had been out searching for food, her fingers blue with cold, her back aching from collecting wood, breaking up the branches and then having to coax the fire to come alive. This all-consuming role of being responsible, being in charge, at the end of everyone's demands, was beginning to make her resentful.

"Anyone can lie in bed and feel sorry for themselves" she screamed inwardly, looking at her mother's still form as she lay there, coveting the only blanket, and listening to the never ending sound of her whining voice. Normally she wanted to protect her mother, help her if she could. But today was different. There was no sun in the sky, no warmth to comfort them and her mother's behaviour finally broke down the barriers. Maria's temper exploded. Losing all control and snatching the blanket away from her mother, she started to shake her violently, shouting and screaming.

"Get out of bed, do something. There's no food, no water.

Look at us - we're cold."

John and Cathy started to cry, frightened at why Maria was shouting at their mother, Ailsa became quiet and with a steely coldness stared at her daughter.

"Then you do something. It's your fault. Everything has always been your fault" she said bitterly. "If it wasn't for you I would be at home now. I'd be happy." Then, turning her back, she took the blanket and wrapped it around herself once again, leaving John and Cathy with nothing.

Maria's whole world stood still, unable to comprehend what her mother had just said. She felt as if she had been hit. Her eyes filled with tears as the two children looked at her questioningly. "No" she whispered quietly in shock. "It isn't true, it can't be."

As young as she was Maria knew it was her father's fault. She knew. So why did her mother think it was her fault? What had she done? She knew her mother didn't like her, but she didn't like John and Cathy either, and what had they ever done? They were only little. She now realised what she had always known. Her mother didn't want her, never had, she didn't belong. At least she knew now, even if she didn't understand why. Her mother blamed her for everything, and those words hurt her more than anything in the whole world.

Taking hold of the kid's hands she pulled them towards her, Maria needed to feel the closeness of her brother and sister. But she also wanted to comfort them, to protect them from ever feeling the way she felt at that moment. They were still frightened, but as Maria held them they relaxed.

"It will be alright" she promised "everything will be alright"

"What about Ma?" John asked. He was frightened at hearing his mother shout at Maria. "You aren't going to leave us are you Maria?"

"No, I promise, I will never go anywhere without you. Cathy as well" she said, looking at her mother's frail little back wrapped in the only blanket they had. She still felt the hurt inside, but she loved her Ma. "We will look after her together John. She's sick, but we will make her better."

"Really" he said. The hopelessness and the fear of the unknown could be heard in the slight tremor of his voice.

Maria smiled "Wait and see." she said, and as much as she wanted to say more, there wasn't anything more she could say. Desperately she wanted to reassure them, she couldn't cope with their sadness or their tears. But Maria also wanted to cry, she wanted to scream at the world and let go of all the hurt she felt herself, but she couldn't. And so her screams remained silently within her. Only the knowledge of revenge gave her strength. As she drew them towards her, held them as she wanted to be held, she knew that the only reason life was like this, was because of him, her father. And now even her mother hated her.

Maria became quiet, thoughtful. Gone was the innocent child who used to believe things would change and everything would be alright. She now knew nothing was going to change. Her mother's words would not go away, they hurt. Someday she would find her father and make him pay, but for now she had two tear-stained faces looking up at her, sad confused little faces.

"Everything is going to be alright." she whispered "I promise"

It was all going to be made right, Maria could feel it. Most of her life she had had feelings about what was going to happen. Not the kind of things where she could see or predict the future, but a kind of sensitivity to the natural forces of life. In the past she had no-one to ask about these feelings and tried to ignore them, but now she embraced them, she needed them, she didn't want to make any mistakes. She was going to take them away and start a new life. She didn't know how but she did know there was no longer any place for tears in her life. In the past her father had ridiculed her, called her ancient names from the past history of his ancestors.

"They were true Gypsies with special gifts" he had said, "and you are nothing but an impostor." He would never admit she was a child of his people, a child who did possess some kind of second sight. But Maria knew she was different. She felt it though she didn't understand it.

Chapter Five.

In the past Maria had been greatly influenced by one of her father's girlfriends. She had said she was going to Manchester in England to start a new life. It was that one sentence which had stayed with her. 'Start a new life'. She didn't want this life, she knew there had to be more to it than this. She wanted more. She wanted more for herself, for John and for Cathy, and especially for her mother.

The following day Maria sold the horse and with the proceeds bought rail tickets. They had never been on a train before. It was all so new and exciting, also very scary. At last the train arrived. Clutching the few belongings they owned, a parcel of food from Anna and Don who had bought the horse from them, they were now ready to board.

"Maria," Don said taking her to one side, "Have you placed the money in different parts of your clothing like I said,"

"Yes," she smiled.

"Good, remember show it no-one, and when you get there, trust no one, no matter how good or helpful they seem to be. Remember this is a city, lots of different kinds of people live there. Some are not honest. Some are just hungry and homeless. They will try and take your money off you, Maria, by whatever means they can. The war has ended, but for some it's still going on. They have lost everything, they live in an empty world."

"I will be careful," she said, not fully understanding what he was saying.

Maria was sure she should have had a birthday but she didn't care. No-one knew what she was like or what she was really capable of. They would see only a child when they knew how old she was. Well that was going to stop right there. She was leaving her age behind her in Scotland.

At five feet four inches she was tall for her age and she knew if she tried hard she could make people accept her as a young woman. After all, fifteen wasn't that far away and yet in terms of living and working it was a whole new life away. One in which she desperately needed. And that was exactly what she was going to have. At fifteen she could apply for work, no-one would question her or tell her what to do. In England her new life would begin as an adult.

Maria closed her eyes, it was as if she was about to enter a whole new world. The life she knew had been left way behind. Her mother, John and Cathy had gone to sleep, but she herself was far too excited. Besides, she had to make sure they didn't miss their connection at Carlisle. It was there they had to change trains for Manchester. The guard at the station had been most helpful. He found them a carriage of their own so they could travel in peace. He had been a youngish man and assumed that the elderly couple who had put them on the train had been their grandparents.

They were now on the biggest adventure of their lives. That was how she had explained it to Cathy and John. They were so excited. Reaching into her pocket, her fingers curled around the small pouch that Anna had given her to put the money in. Don had given her the money to take charge of.

"I know you are young Maria, but I think you are probably the most responsible one to have it." He had said gravely. Maria felt terribly grown up.

It was a beautiful carriage. The seats were covered in a rich red and green fabric with real wood panels on the wall. Maria was fascinated. Even the windows had curtains. She couldn't help herself, she had to pull them together then open them again, tying them back with a lovely red piece of cord on a golden hook. They were beautiful.

Returning to the window, looking at the changing scenery of the countryside, she felt strangely alive. Her heart was beating faster yet she was relaxed. Everything was so new. She saw her reflection in the window as they entered a tunnel.

"Where are we going?" she whispered quietly," where is life taking us?"

Her dark eyes sparkled, as they stared silently back.

They changed trains and were now on their way to Manchester. The guards had been wonderful. Maria was learning fast. People felt sorry for them, offering help and advice. The guard told her about Manchester and how it was a very large city, people from all over the country including immigrants lived there. Maria didn't know what an immigrant was but decided not to interrupt him. He was going into great detail about the poverty, crime and destruction that had happened during and after the war. Suddenly, Manchester seemed more like a nightmare than a new and exciting life. She was beginning to doubt her decision. Had she done the right thing? What else could they do? No, she decided, she wasn't going to let anyone put her off. It was her dream and she would make it happen. She had heard before of the poverty, but she had also heard of the work and the money that could be made. Maria knew she was going to succeed and find a way. She just knew.

It was April and very cold. The children huddled together

to keep warm as the train rattled towards the station. They were almost there. The impact of what she had done came to Maria with the full force of impending doom. It was the sight of row upon row of small dirty houses that flashed by the window. She had never seen anything like it. She could also see the apprehension in the faces of her mother, Cathy and John. It was unbelievable. There were no open spaces, no countryside, nothing. Only war-torn buildings wherever you looked, dejected and broken. Everywhere people seemed to be living on derelict land, all hovering around crude camp fires in an attempt to keep warm. She could feel her heart thundering inside her chest.

Maria hesitated; fear seemed to overcome her as she stepped from the train onto the platform. Keeping them together she slowly made her way to the exit. She had never seen so many people. They all crammed into the same spot going the same way. No one seemed to care if they knocked you, banged you or pushed into you. The four of them were overwhelmed. It was Maria who brought them all down back to earth.

"We have to hold on to each other because if we don't, and you get lost, I will never be able to find you."

John grabbed his mother's hand and held onto Maria's coat as well, frightened at the thought she had just planted onto his head.

Together they trundled down the road, leaving the train station and its people behind. Maria could see poverty everywhere she looked. People lived in shop doorways, and children cried from hunger and the cold. Many held out their small hands begging for a few pence from the many passers-by, but not many stopped, most just hung their head low and carried on. Maria didn't feel anything for them, she just knew she would have to do better than they had. She had to be stronger and find a place to live so she could look after her family. Somehow, without realising it, Maria had taken on complete responsibility for them all. It was as she had promised herself, her childhood had gone and she was now an adult in Manchester.

Ailsa complained to her daughter, she was tired of walking and wanted to know where she was taking them. John and Cathy whimpered in the cold asking again and again "Are we there yet?" "Nearly" Maria would answer, showing none of the anxiety she was feeling. She didn't know where they were going but she wasn't going to tell them that. She had, after all, been living on her instincts all her life, she wasn't about to doubt them now.

Leaving the centre of Manchester they continued to walk down Great Ducie Street, then on to Bury New Road. Maria read the names of the road and realised all the shop windows displayed cards advertising rooms to let, and most of the addresses were on or off Bury New Road in an area called Strangeways. Maria took this as an omen as nothing could be as strange as the way their life had changed and brought them to this exact spot. She copied down one of the addresses.

Eventually they came to Waterloo Road and looking down at the piece of paper, she checked it, and then turned into a small street. The houses were all joined onto one another with no gardens. There was no sign of trees, flowers or animals except for the odd stray dog. But there were lots of people, people of all ages, who seemed to stand out onto the street in small groups talking. Many of them spoke in languages and accents she couldn't understand. One thing though, that they did have in common, was the fact they all looked poor.

This was so different to what they had been used to, the

open roads, fields, the hills and the meadows. And now this, it was so overwhelming Maria fought to hold back the tears. It even smelt strange. Her mother stared blankly at the terraced house before her.

"Is this the best you can do?" she said flatly. Ailsa could see Maria was struggling but she didn't care, nothing touched her because she knew she couldn't help even if she wanted to, she didn't know how.

"No" Maria answered, knocking on the door, "And we only have one room here not the house. One look from Maria stopped her mother from saying anything more.

The door opened and a large overweight lady stood there dressed in the most garish dress they had ever seen. Her white hair was held back by a broken clasp which let long strands of hair escape wistfully around one side of her face. She had a round face with full lips which hung in a very sad smile; her pale eyes were almost green. Maria could hardly speak for looking at her.

"Come for a room then?" she directed at Ailsa.

"Yes, if you have one" Maria answered.

"Got one family room on the ground floor, interested?"

Maria nodded, and pushing John and Cathy in front followed with her mother as they were shown the room. It was cold and damp; a large bay window with no curtains brought in the light but it was draughty enough to freeze anything. One large double bed covered the wall opposite the window, two chairs and a table stood against the other wall which had a small dresser in the corner with three drawers.

There was a large open fireplace where you could do your cooking and warm the place well. This was the total comfort of the room. There was an outside lavatory and a small scullery with running water that everyone in the house could share.

"This is it then, our new life?" Ailsa said.

The kids could feel her depression, but Maria said it was better than the caravan, at least they had a large bed where they could all sleep. Cathy and John agreed as they jumped up and down on the bed, Maria made a fire and produced the bread and jam she had bought. As the fire blazed and they made toast, the warmth from the fire and the comfort of a hot drink made Maria truly believe they were going to be happy.

Fed, warm and a big bed to sleep in. The knowledge that the room was theirs and only theirs brought great relief and they had the best sleep they had had for a long time. She knew they would be comfortable here in time, but where was she was going to find the money for the rent? She had been shocked at how much Ada the owner, had taken off them for one week. Maria knew the little bit of money that Don McGregor had given them would not last very long if she had to pay the rent and buy food out of it. Ada lived in the room next door, she seemed helpful but her ma wouldn't let her in, said she was interfering and would always try to poke her nose into something that had nothing to do with her. Maria knew that they needed help. It was alright for her mother to refuse to talk to anyone, but that didn't solve anything. The money Ada asked for was just for one week, where was the money going to come from to pay it every week and what about the food?

Chapter Six.

There was only one person they could go to for help, and that was Ada. They didn't know anybody else. Maria had no choice, but how would she ask? She knew Ada had borne four children. They had all died in the war and Ada was still mourning them. Maria had heard her telling the lady who lived upstairs.

"Ada" she said quietly trying to find some courage, "me Ma's sick and can't work yet and we only have a little money, and I don't know where to go to get more rent for you. You won't throw us out will you? "As much as Maria wanted to be strong, her voice gave way to the terror she was feeling inside. If they were to be actually thrown on the streets with nowhere to go, what would happen to them then? Maria wished she could have the luxury of being able to cry sometimes.

Ada stood and looked at the thin child in front of her. "Almost waif like" she thought "The child was strong, there was no doubt about that, but was she strong enough to look after the rest of them?" Ada wasn't sure what she should do. Inform the authorities? No, she decided, the kid needed help not hassle. It wasn't normal to see so much sadness in the eyes of a child, she deserved a break. Whatever had happened in her short life was there staring out at her, but there was also a hardness and a protectiveness Ada hadn't seen for a long time, it somehow reminded her of when she had her own family around her. What she would give to be able to have them back.

"Where's your father, child?" she asked

Maria wanted to tell her the truth, of how he just walked

out and abandoned his family leaving them with nothing, but instead decided that was something only they should know, no-one else. Maria hated being like this, she didn't like telling lies; she was convinced it brought bad luck. This was all his fault, she couldn't wait to grow up and find him.

"He never came back from the war." She lied, with a tear in her eye.

Ada was instantly sorry for this little tragic family. Having lost her own family she thought she understood the pain they were feeling.

"You need to go down to the National Assistance Board. That's a Government Department where they help people like your mother."

"What do they do?" Maria always had it at the back of her mind what her father had threatened them with. They would all be taken away.

"They will ask you for proof of who you all are, so you will need to take your birth certificates and your mother's marriage certificate with you, does your mother have them?"

"I don't know."

"Don't look so worried, they are there to help you. Come on, I'll help you find what we need." Ada said confidently.

Maria hesitated.

"Ma don't like anyone to come in "she said

"Well at this moment, we will have to ignore what your ma says, because she will have to make the claim and get some money,"

"Can we really, I mean get some money?"

Ada smiled at Maria, she was so young, her mother was sick and Ada knew it wasn't the kind of sickness you recovered from. The child had a lot on her plate.

"You'll get enough for the rent, the coal and to buy food. Your ma will be given a payment book. It's not a lot but it's enough. You then take it to the Post Office on the High Street every week and they will pay you whatever is written in the book."

Maria felt so relieved she wanted to throw her arms around her, instead she smiled, opened the door quietly and they went in. John and Cathy were shocked to see Maria bringing in the lady from next door, and even more surprised when she beckoned them not to say a word as they went over to the bed where mother was sleeping and pulled the wooden box from under the bed. Ada put it on the table and together with Maria, went through the papers taking out the ones she thought that she would need.

"Tomorrow I will take you down; your mother will have to come though, she will be the one that has to make the claim" she repeated.

Maria hesitated; she knew what her mother was like.

"Don't worry, I will come in, in the morning and make sure she comes." Ada said knowing what Maria was thinking.

The next day found them all walking down the road. Ada, true to her word, had come in and got Ailsa out of bed, dressed her, and told her she had to come or she would be living on the streets. That seemed to make her move, it instilled some sort of fear inside her mind. Quietly she allowed herself to be dressed and then duly found herself walking down the road with Ada, Maria and the two young ones. After what seemed like an eternity to her they arrived. Maria standing beside her mother, prompting her, helped answer all the questions needed to make a claim. Ailsa signed the relevant forms, happy at Maria's reason for her missing husband, the people had treated her with respect and it felt good, it had been so long since she felt like that. She smiled thankfully at the young lady and left with her family and neighbour to wait and receive the much needed and appreciated money.

Later that night though, when they were all asleep in bed Maria could hear her mother talking to herself in her sleep, she had not done that lately, Maria didn't mind though, she was glad, it was nice just to hear her voice even if it wasn't directed at them. Tonight though it was more like a nightmare, her mother's voice rose and fell, sometimes Maria could hear her other times she couldn't. But she couldn't understand most things.

Then she would cry, soft pitying cries, but Maria couldn't feel sorry for her, she felt so much anger inside, she thought it would explode. The same questions repeated themselves over and over in her head, "Why was she always crying? Why doesn't she shout, get angry at the one who has done this to us, the one who treated her so badly? Maria blamed him for everything and looking at her mother, knew she would never forgive him.

Once the money was sorted, life felt more stable, more secure. Her mother still slept most of the time, but Ada did try and get her up, occasionally she succeeded, but other times she knew she was wasting her time. Ada, having read all the private information on Maria's birth certificate, realised how old she really was.

"You can be any age you want to be, it has nothing to do with anyone"

"Really?" Maria exclaimed.

"Really. Except the authorities. You will have to go to school."

Maria felt deflated.

"I don't want to, I can read and write and I want to work and earn money."

"Fine, but if you don't go to school you will be picked up and put in an institution, that's a large home for children, and there they will keep you until you are fifteen. And then what would happen to Cathy and John? Your mother can't look after them. You only have three more years to go. Make the most of it; learn all you can because if you want to get on in this world, you have to be educated."

Again, Maria's world was taking another turn. She felt so frustrated. She didn't want to go to school. Why was everything so hard? There was no reason why she should have to go, she knew everything she wanted to know, but what really hurt was the fact she couldn't play the role of a grownup. She was so looking forward to finding a job, it would have opened up a whole new world, but instead she felt it all crumble away. School was going to take away her dream and she really resented it. The only good thing was the timing, they were now in May and it would soon be summer and the schools were preparing to close. It made a strong argument to delay going.

Maria talked her way into getting Ada to agree with her. Her mother wasn't interested, but Maria was a little unsure of what Ada would do if she didn't go to school. Ada said she would get into trouble as well, and she wasn't having any of that. But for the moment Maria was happy she had all the summer to look forward to without school. She even thought, she may be lucky enough to get a little job, then her life would really be good.

Chapter Seven.

Sometimes when she wanted to be alone, Maria would wander on down to the banks of the River Irwell, it wasn't too far away and for the most part was quite deserted and was the perfect place to sit and think with no distractions. She considered it to be her own private space and no one was welcome. Except, for the last few days a dark haired boy had started to appear. He also sat on the embankment alone, unaware of his surroundings or if anyone was there. Maria used to watch him slowly, quietly. He reminded her of herself. He was always sad and never with anyone. She felt a strange closeness to him, as if they had both shared the same horrible life that had been given them, with no good reasons of pleasure to help them understand or have anything to enjoy.

Except for his picnic box, that is. He always had a box full of food. Maria would watch him eating when she thought he wasn't looking. His food looked different but smelt heavenly, she was really envious. Firstly because he had food, but more than that was the fact he had someone who looked after him, someone who took pains to make sure he had something good to eat. So why was he always sad? She couldn't understand it. He was older than her, she guessed about seventeen. He was really a man, she thought, but men don't sit by rivers on their own eating lunch.

Today though he smiled, he had lovely teeth and Maria thought how handsome he looked when he did. He really did remind her of herself with large brown eyes, dark skin and thick black hair, but he wore a strange looking small round hat on his head always. Intense curiosity made Maria really want to know why, but how could she ask him? As she had never spoken to him, it would be a bit difficult.

She returned his smile and left to go back home knowing she'd be back again and they would become friends. Maria always trusted her feelings and he was going to become part of her life, she knew it. With a spring in her step she went home, she had never had a friend before and couldn't wait for it to happen.

Several days later, Maria was feeling unusually down, wondering what she was supposed to be doing in life, because she really didn't know. There was no one to ask. Ada had told her, her ma was sick, the kind of sickness you get in the mind, just as bad as being sick in the body only harder to understand. Maria had asked if she would get better but Ada said she didn't know.

Maria didn't want her life to be always like this, even if she couldn't compare it with anyone else's. She remembered the books she read once, the one showing her the big house with lots of wonderful things. She sighed, wanting to know how you got one of them, and even though she had the ambition, and the determination to succeed, she still had her family and there was nobody to help her, and she had to admit as hard as it was, she was still young. And with it came the unknown, the inability to plan because she didn't know how the world worked. She knew only hate for her father. In the past she blamed her mother for being weak, but now after what Ada had said, she didn't blame her anymore, but she was disappointed that she could no longer hope for her to get better and help look after Cathy and John.

So Maria sat, staring into the grey murky waters of the river Irwell, deep in thought, unaware of the dark eyes that watched her. It was David, the young man with the picnic box who Maria would normally be looking out for. Watching her face David's heart went out to her, he had never seen so much pain and sorrow in a young girl.

"Hi" he said quietly

Maria felt as though she had been in a trance and had just awoken from it, she looked up.

"I'm David," he said simply.

"Maria"

"We've been nearly meeting for weeks" he smiled.

"Yes" she answered almost in a whisper.

Sitting beside her like it was the most natural thing in the world. He opened his picnic box and offered to share it with Maria. At first she refused, trying to be polite, but David, totally at ease, soon had her relaxed and smiling. As they ate together, the sandwiches, cake and fruit, Maria thought she had never tasted such wonderful food.

"Are you rich?" she asked before realising it was wrong to do so.

"No" he said with a kind of melancholy.

Sensing his feelings, Maria decided to talk about her little family and a little of her life, not much, and then remained quiet until he was ready to speak. He seemed so sad.

"My aunt looks after me" he said eventually, "My uncle owns a factory, just a small one,"

Maria still remained quiet, waiting for him to talk about his mum and dad or if he had any brothers or sisters.

After what seemed like an eternity David finally spoke.

"I'm Jewish." He said simply.

Maria didn't know what Jewish meant.

"You don't understand do you?"

"No"

"Well you are a Christian aren't you?"

"Yes"

"Well as you believe in Christianity, I am Jewish and I believe in my religion. Have you heard much about what went on in the war?"

"No"

"Well a lot of terrible things went on, including the murder of many thousands of Jewish people." He paused unable to go on.

"Your family, were they....."

"My mother and father, two brothers and a sister, there is only me left. I was the lucky one. My aunt smuggled me out of the country and brought me to England."

Maria remained silent not knowing what to say. So many emotions were racing through her body which she didn't understand.

David suddenly smiled, that half smile he did which made Maria respond instantly.

"Here have some kosher food" he said lightening the conversation.

"What's kosher?"

"I can see I will have to educate you," he smiled "It's what Jewish people eat."

She wanted to ask him where he came from, but knew this wasn't the time, instead she just laughed softly saying it was the best food she had ever tasted.

David felt really close to Maria, he didn't know why; she was obviously younger than him, and a girl, and also someone who knew very little about life. But whatever it was, he felt the need to talk. Something he hadn't been able to do for so long. Whether it was her innocence or honesty or the fact she seemed to understand the pain of life he didn't know. But whatever it was, he spoke about things he had never spoken about before, and afterwards realised a bond so strong had grown between them it could never be broken.

At long last Maria had found a friend. She was so happy she couldn't believe it. To have someone to talk to and share her thoughts and her feelings with, was something she never thought she would ever have. He just happened to be a wonderful person, honest and handsome and had an overwhelming love for his family. Plus he liked her. To Maria, he was the most perfect person she would ever meet. Her own problems paled into insignificance next to his. Having no knowledge of war or death and not really understanding it, she could only see and feel the pain that he felt but it was that closeness that made Maria feel part of his life.

Chapter Eight.

David soon realised he loved her. Maria may be a child, but she possessed a maturity way past most women. She understood him more than anyone he knew. He also saw the love in her eyes, a love she wanted to show but didn't. He admired her strength and passion for the family she cared so deeply for.

They met often, he would share his lunch and they would sit contented, both learning how to laugh and talk about nothing. It gave them a sense of freedom of which they had both forgotten. So for a few hours a week, they enjoyed being like any other young couple. They put their troubles aside and relaxed, and enjoyed the moments they spent together.

The days passed quickly, but it was on one such day as they sat together each happy in their own space that David brought her back to reality. It was when she said she was going to get a job because she needed the money.

"But you will have to go to school," he said.

"No, I don't need to, besides I have to start saving, I promised"

"What did you promise Maria?"

"I promised I would take everyone back to Scotland, to the place where my mother came from."

"Well I'm sure you will one day, but you still have to go to school it's the law."

"But I don't need to."

David loved her innocence. If only life were that simple.

"Well you will have to, you don't have a choice. It really is the law, and anyway, my father always said if you are to succeed and be what you want to be, then learn from life, but just as important learn from school, get your education."

"Do you believe him?"

David stared at her, she wasn't being insulting or doubting his word, she just couldn't understand how you could listen to someone and actually live your life according to their advice.

"Maria, you and your brother and sister have to go to school, it will be for the best, believe me"

"Do you go to school?"

"I did. King David's. I'm too old now"

"That's your name"

"Yes, but there's no connection, honest," he smiled.

Maria grinned. She loved it when he smiled at her.

David decided he would try and help her, to see if there was any way she could get into the world of earning money, even though he thought it was wrong that she was being forced into it. Still, she only needed to earn a little to begin with, then maybe she would relax, and enjoy life. But somehow he kind of knew that wouldn't be the case; there was something inside her he hadn't quite figured out. It was as if she was filled with a silent emotion she couldn't release. He was drawn to her and hoped someday she would confide in him, and whatever it was, she would let it all out.

The only thing Maria feared in life was fire. So when David suggested a little job, it was with some trepidation she asked John to help her. David explained that because of religious beliefs, some families couldn't put coal on the fire on the Sabbath and needed help. And so every Friday night and Saturday morning, Maria, along with John, soon built up a large number of people who needed them. Some even paid them for switching the light on. Every penny helped. At first, John thought he should get paid, but Maria soon explained to him quietly and made him promise not to tell anyone. It was their secret. She said she was going to take them all home, just like their mother wanted. John was so happy, his soft smile spread across his face and his eyes lit up with excitement.

"Oh Maria really, can we go, honest?" his face beamed.

"Yes John, we can but it really is our secret. I don't know how long or how much money it will take, but we will get there, I promise. We will just have to work very hard and one day we will all be happy. But John, don't tell anyone at school will you, about us earning money, they might take it from us."

"Why?" he asked.

Because when I took Ma to that place to get money, remember the one Ada told us about."

"Yes" he answered, trying desperately to remember.

"Well we had to say we had no money and no work. That's

why Ma gets money to give Ada for the rent, and buy food from the shop. We don't want that to be stopped do we?"

"I promise, cross my heart" he said, "I won't talk to anyone ever again."

Maria smiled at his face trying so hard to be serious, but she knew she could trust him. And so they continued all through the summer.

Chapter Nine.

Maria hated school. There was nothing she could remotely identify with. It was a place full of stupid rules which made no sense and kids that were cruel and unfriendly. As they hurried to school one morning very aware of the impending storm she desperately tried to get John and Cathy to hurry even more. Because no matter how hard she tried, she just couldn't get there on time.

This day was particularly cold and dark. Mr.Burgen from the local shop looked up hoping the rain would hold off until he finished unloading his van of the many boxes of fruit. It was then as the children passed his eyes suddenly filled up. He was used to poverty, it was all around him. But he thought there was something almost tragic about those kids. He watched them as they hurried to school, unwashed, unkempt, wearing threadbare clothes which hung loosely on their thin little bodies, and shoes that were held together with elastic bands. They looked so pathetic, as they each clung to the other. The older one pleading for them to go faster, but he knew they couldn't, the ground was wet and uneven and the youngest had already fallen once.

Maria was the eldest; her long dark hair hung in untidy wet curls, her face unwashed her eyes sad. Today she was almost in tears. She desperately wanted to be early. John was seven and tried so hard for her, but Cathy was only four and her legs ached. She was tired and hungry and didn't want to go to school. She wanted to stay at home, to curl up in bed with her mother and feel warm. Cathy blamed Maria, she didn't understand. She didn't understand anything anymore.

"Don't want to go to school." She wailed, "It's all your fault. Ma said I could stay at home. She said I could stay in bed and be warm. But you won't let me."

Maria felt the tears prickle behind her eyes.

"Why did we have to come here anyway?"

Maria sighed, Cathy had tears in her eyes and John looked tired. Had she done the right thing? She didn't know. Manchester was a strange place, unfriendly, overcrowded and where everyone spoke in different languages. She hated sharing an old house with strangers, but most of all she hated how Ma was so sick she couldn't get out of bed anymore.

The three children arrived at the entrance of the old grey building marked 'Infant school'. The two younger ones scurried through the door as the rain threatened to cascade down in heavy torrents. Maria ran towards the door marked 'junior school' but she was too late. The rain caught her. Unable to escape from the severity of the downpour she stood there drenched. Looking down at her clothes as they dripped water all over the highly polished floor, she was terrified. Her tears mingled with the rain, her lips tasting the salt as she wiped them away with her sleeve.

"Please God, no, not again." She cried, as her legs took her along the corridor against her will. It was a large, old, dilapidated building, dark and dismal. It had tall heavy wooden panels that screened both sides of the walls on the corridor. Large statues appeared to be looking down on her as she passed slowly by. She paused beneath the statue of Our Lady who held the Infant Jesus in her arms. To her, this statue was the only friendly one around. The others frightened her. She looked deep into the eyes of the face that peered back, willing it to do something.

"Help me" she whispered.

39

Maria felt the pain of hunger and despair. She saw no answers and didn't really know the right questions. Tired and exhausted, she paused to look around. Of all the schools she had been to, and there had been many, this one had to be the worst. Because no matter how hard she tried, she just couldn't get there on time. Trying to push her private thoughts aside she shoved her hands deeper into her pockets, determined not to think of what was in front of her, but it was hard. She knew exactly what was in front of her.

"Punctuality is one of the most important things in life, if you are to succeed, be early at all times, there are no excuses, no reasons. And if you are late, a cane will be administered." This was the writing on the wall as she entered the building. She knew it off by heart, every single word, every syllable.

Maria shivered with the cold as she walked down the long corridor with the wooden floors. She could hear her shoes squelching, feel the icy water that seeped through the holes with each step she took, and there was nothing she could do. She couldn't hide it, the evidence was there for all to see as a long wet trail followed her.

With a heavy heart she also knew the worst was yet to come. She was on her way to the head teacher's office, again, for being late. Despair overwhelmed her as did the injustices of life, she desperately wanted to run away and never come back, but she couldn't. Instead she wiped the tears from her face, straightened her wet coat, then knocked on the door.

"Enter"

She heard the voice of Miss Jay the Head teacher. She was a softly spoken woman, who wore long flowing black clothes tied together with numerous coloured beads around the neck. Her hair was as fair, as her clothes were dark, framing her delicate face with quiet curls. Everyone loved her she was always smiling, that is, unless you were late. Then out came the cane.

Twice a day, every day, Maria was caned. Always it missed her tiny outstretched fingers, landing instead firmly across her wrist. At first Maria cried out, but then the tears dried up as did the pain. She would just stand there, silently looking at the two large angry welts which spread across her wrists. They had appeared on the first day and had never had a chance to heal. She knew what was coming, so she would just stand and look defiantly into the eyes of her principal, hold out her hand and wait for the punishment she knew she didn't deserve.

"Well, I don't care." She would think in defiance.

And so she would continue to stare, her young hostility shining through those large dark eyes with the perfect oval shape, as Miss Jay's long thin cane came down in that oh so familiar rhythm that brought the pain.

But Maria wouldn't acknowledge pain, her face was set like stone, her eyes piercing and unemotional. Her usual quiet way had given her the reputation of being naughty and that soon progressed to lots of stronger words, some of which she didn't understand, but was left in no doubt what they meant. Because they were relatively new in the area most people didn't know them, and with their mother very rarely going out and Maria being quiet, no one really took the trouble to ask why she was always late. Maria, now classed as disruptive, disobedient, and generally a very insolent girl who flaunted the rules of the school, wished she could belong but didn't know how.

Then one day her prayers were answered, there was to be a reading test, and this was the one thing she knew she was good at. It was something she loved. Teaching her to read was probably the only thing her father had ever done for her. And that was done purely for selfish reasons. But she was happy reading, it allowed her into other people's worlds. It allowed her to know the world she was going to live in.

Today she would show them all, she would prove she wasn't stupid. Poor, dirty even, but not stupid. At last she heard her name called. This was it, her moment in time to show them all. She stood confidently and took a deep breath. Maria hated being the centre of attention as she was now with all eyes on her. But she knew she could do it, she had to. This was her one chance to prove herself. Taking the book offered to her she turned to the page she was to read, she knew she was at a disadvantage with the other children because they had been reading it all year, and had in fact moved on from it. And this was before Maria had even started at the school.

Slowly and clearly she began to read.

"Start again and this time, do it correctly," The teacher interrupted irritably. "Will you concentrate child."

Maria thought she must have made a mistake because she was nervous, she started again, trying to read more slowly and her words more clearly. But again the teacher interrupted her, this time becoming agitated with Maria's efforts of trying to read. Maria felt her lip begin to tremble as she looked at the page. She was reading it correctly, she was doing everything right. So why was she being treated like this? Her whole being was in danger of crumbling as her mind struggled to understand what was happening. She tried one more time to read the passage, aware of the whispering and sniggering that was now going on all around her. Eyes openly staring as though she had suddenly developed two heads. Maria became nervous.

She dropped the book. It landed on the floor with a loud crack.

It was in that instance Maria saw Miss Moynihan, her face red with temper, someone Maria had always thought of as a little grey haired old lady had suddenly become a monster. Her eyes were flashing wildly, and her lips had disappeared into a thin hard line, but it was her nostrils that frightened her most. They flared so wide they looked totally unreal.

"Insolent brat" she screamed as Maria felt the full force of her hand across her face.

The class became deathly quiet; they had never experienced anything like this before, why Miss Moynihan had never ever raised her voice let alone shouted. The idea of Miss Moynihan actually striking a child would never have been believed.

Maria was in shock, unable to move, she didn't know what to do or what had happened, she stood and silently cried.

Trying to compose what little bit of dignity she had left, Miss Moynihan was struggling to believe she had actually lost her temper to such an extent, as to strike a child. It was just too much for her rational mind to accept. Trying to salvage what had become a complete disaster she turned to Maria.

"Please pick up the book" she said in a very quiet controlled voice.

All eyes watched, waited to see if she would, Maria's face was ashen except for the angry red finger marks across her right cheek. But it was in her eyes that she seemed so different. Inside she had wanted to read so badly it had hurt. And now that dream of proving herself had disappeared.

Sadness so great seemed to have wrapped itself around her. Gone were all her expectations. Inside, she felt cold and empty.

Maria slowly handed the book back, no longer caring what happened, but as her teacher opened the book at the chosen page she visibly gasped in shock. For a moment Maria thought Miss Moynihan was going to cry, her face had crumpled, and her skin had paled.

"I'm so terribly sorry Maria," she said, the anguish clearly heard in her voice. Taking her hand, she gently led Maria to the front of the class. "We owe Maria an apology," she said, in full view of everybody "the book she was reading from, is in fact, an older version from last term. I'm sorry Maria, it looks the same, but it's different to the one the rest of us in class have. It must have got mixed up somehow. But you wouldn't know that, because you weren't here last year. I truly am sorry." she said emotionally.

Everyone waited, including Miss Moynihan for a reaction, but none came. Maria was tired of being hurt.

Chapter Ten.

David proved to be a good friend to Maria, he was always there supporting her and helping, giving advice, although sometimes he did have to confer with his family. But they never questioned him about his new friend. They only said the world was about people, about friends and trust and this was something you could only learn by being yourself.

Maria worked hard and never complained she loved the area called Strangeways. She felt so much a part of Jewish life, this was because of David. He had the kind of family life she yearned for, the total togetherness of their culture, bound together by their belief and love. She desperately wanted to be part of that, to belong.

As time passed, Maria realised just how much she had come to feel for him. David had become the stability her young life wanted; he gave her the strength and support she so desperately needed. She knew David would always be there for her. He understood her, understood poverty and responsibility and the loneliness of having no-one. She knew there was no future with him, but that didn't stop her from dreaming. She loved him, but she also knew she couldn't tell him. Young as she was, she fully understood the implications and the unhappiness it would bring. Their friendship might never be the same, and she couldn't cope with that. The thought of life without him was unbearable. No, her love for now had to be her secret alone, though it silently broke her heart.

David and his family helped Maria grow into maturity, teaching her the rights and wrongs of life and how to deal with people she didn't understand. They tried to teach her how to forgive, but she found that hard to understand. There were good days, days when David would take them out for a walk. Maria remembered the first time he had taken them all to Heaton park. She was so happy it was like being in the country. Something they had all missed terribly.

Large rhododendron bushes in pink, purple, lilac and white were everywhere, their soft petals coming together to make large balls of flowers, that sat complementing the deep evergreen leaves of the bush. The scent was overpowering, but not as much as its abundance of beauty as every path was laden with overhanging branches. It was as if you could get lost in its beauty and forever feel the luxury of nature. It was paradise; David stopped, his hands out stretched.

"Well," he said, "Is it as good as I promised?"

"Oh it's more" Maria whispered.

"It's brilliant!" cried John as he kept disappearing in and out of the bushes.

Even Cathy was smiling as she fingered the soft petals.

"There are so many" she said her little face shining with happiness.

David looked at all their faces he was so glad he brought them, it was good to see them so happy. It had been his Aunt's idea.

"Take them to the park," she said, "Let them feel nature again, they have probably forgotten what rolling hills and grass look like. And don't forget to take them down the paths through the rhododendron bushes"

She had been so right. Their faces couldn't hide the sheer pleasure of seeing once again wide open spaces filled with the many wonderful colours of flowers, trees and bushes.

"Let's stop here," David said.

And opening his bag produced a white cloth on which he proceeded to place small packages of food.

"I don't want this day to end, ever," Cathy said as he offered her some food.

"Can we come again?" John asked.

But Maria was too full of emotion to even speak. She was so happy, happier than she had ever been in her whole life, and looking at David, she also wished this day would never end.

There were many outings after that and each time David found them something new to see in the park. But for Maria the best place had to be when they were beside the lake. Sitting in silence amongst the trees, watching Cathy and John, each happy in their own thoughts.

Maria could feel his love, and when they accidentally touched, or brushed slightly together or when he pointed to the ducks and she had turned round quickly and their lips almost touched. Maria realised that the most powerful emotion you can feel is sometimes when there is no actual bodily contact. But your heart races and your body feels weak with anticipation and a longing you know, will one day be satisfied.

Chapter Eleven.

Maria realised her mother's illness was getting worse when one day in a fit of depression she took the scissors and cut Cathy's hair off. Cathy screamed and cried and refused to go out. Maria shouted, but Ailsa just went back to bed as if nothing had happened, she couldn't understand what all the fuss was about.

Maria continued to work but realised she needed something that paid a little more money or she would never have enough to take them back to Scotland where they wanted to be. She just hoped when the time came her grandparents would accept them. But underneath she didn't really believe it. She only knew that unless she took them back she would have to look after her mother for the rest of her life, and though she loved her she knew she couldn't do it.

Maturity seemed to happen overnight, she became a strong independent young woman of fourteen. Not pretty, but extremely attractive and womanly. Thick dark waves shone in abundance as her unruly hair cascaded down her back. Almond shaped eyes deep set and shaded by long heavy dark lashes, seemed to entice you to look into them, it was as though they held the mysteries of life. Her face was not that of a traditional beauty, her nose was probably too large, and her lips too wide, but they were well defined lips of a true natural red. And the shape of her face brought it all together, good high cheekbones, a strong jaw line and a long slender neck placed on the shoulders of a body any woman would be proud of. Full rounded, feminine, a slim waist that accentuated the curves of her hips and long shapely legs. Maria was to all intents a very beautiful woman in a wild sort of way, but with an innocence that drew you to her.

The following weeks were much the same except life was

more relaxed, maybe it was because she now had a purpose in life - to take them home. Or maybe it was because one day she wouldn't have to look after them all and could spend more time with David. The only thing that frightened her was that David wouldn't wait until she was older, and she could tell him how she really felt. She refused to understand the implications of a Jewish boy marrying a Catholic, she only knew she loved him, he was the only person in the whole world she wanted to spend her life with. It was for him as much as for her own ambitions that she worked so hard at school.

It was on a cold wet Monday afternoon that Maria's life came tumbling down yet again. She was on her way to the shops when she saw David coming towards her. She knew something was wrong, his shoulders stooped, his eyes were downcast. Suddenly she felt panic rise inside her.

"Good news," he said trying to smile as he approached her.

"There is a job going in a small handbag factory, it will be ideal for you, no questions asked and it is only five minutes away from where you live."

It was good news but Maria wanted to know what the matter was, she had never seen him so sad looking, well, not since she had first met him.

"What's to do?" she asked almost frightened of the answer.

"I have to go away"

"Oh," was all she could say.

"Yes, I am to meet my bride, my future wife."

As the full impact of what he had just said penetrated her brain she wanted to scream. She wanted to believe she was hearing things, it couldn't be true. But it was as though a cold steel blade had pierced her heart. She couldn't speak, tears cascaded down her face as she lost control in a sea of pain.

"You can't," she eventually whispered.

"Please Maria, don't make it any harder than it is." Although it had never been said, he knew she loved him. What she didn't know was that he felt the same.

"I owe my aunt my life, the least I can do is marry a girl of her choice, and she wants me to do this so that it will bring two families together again. After the wedding, Sarah, that's her name, will be able to come to England and be reunited with her family, with the people she loves and needs to be with. It is my duty. She is a young Jewish girl and will be an excellent partner for me."

Maria felt as though her whole world had collapsed, she loved him so much. She had never said anything to him, but had always dreamt that one day they would be together. That dream had now gone, and she had never felt such pain. Her heart felt as though it were broken and the pain inside ripped her apart. Then she was angry, she hurt badly but she also felt betrayed.

"Hope you'll be happy."

"Maria"

"No, it's alright honest, I can't wait to grow up and marry a nice Catholic boy."

She wanted to hurt him, as she was feeling hurt now. She knew it was childish but didn't know what else to do.

"I'll write," he said sadly, "I will always think of you."

"Yeah, sure"

"Really I will, and anyway, I am only going for two years."

"Then what, I meet the family?"

"Please Maria, try to understand."

But she remained silent. Two years was a life time away. Staring up into his eyes she saw his pain and something else. Was it love? Did he love her? He couldn't, because if he did, she reasoned, he wouldn't be walking away. She watched him go and in that instance she grew up, knew the pain of rejection from one she loved so dearly, for this was clearly the greatest, rejection. To Maria, if you wanted to do something in life, then you did it. After all, it was your life to do with as you wished, and David, she thought, must really have wanted to marry Sarah.

Chapter Twelve.

Throwing herself into her new job at the handbag factory, Maria pushed herself on and on, relentless in her task to earn money and to put David out of her mind. Most of the time she just got on with her job refusing to form any kind of a close relationship, or friendships with anyone. At first it was because she didn't want anyone to know her age, but as time passed, she realised it was because most of the workers were just passing through, illegal most of them, from different countries, all trying to survive. Everyone learnt to survive, you didn't ask questions. However, this in turn led to a lot of distrust and flagrant disrespect of one another. There were only a few that had actually been there as long as Maria.

This new influx of workers brought unwelcome attention from some of the younger male ones. They used to watch Maria closely. She could stimulate them without even knowing. Simply because she didn't know she was doing anything and knew nothing of how men felt or what they thought. In fact she knew nothing about that part of life; her mother never spoke to her, unless it was to complain. And so Maria didn't know how to react when she received unwelcome attention.

It was dark, the day had come to a close and everyone was leaving. Maria tidied her bench, placing the handbags in different boxes, half-finished ones and ones that were finished waiting to be bagged all had their place. When suddenly, she had a feeling something was wrong, tension was in the air, mixed with a quiet fear that started to envelope her. She turned around but saw no one. "Must be all in the mind," she muttered. But then she saw the shadows, her own light flicked off and she knew there was more than one person there. For the first time in her young life she felt truly frightened.

She heard the key turn in the door. She was locked in, but with whom? Suddenly they were there, hands tearing at her clothes, pulling her down, she could hear her dress ripping, feel cold hands exploring down into her skin. She fought, kicked, but there was more than one of them. Her teeth bit deep into the hand that was trying to cover her mouth, and in that split second as he pulled away, she screamed.

It was as if all the pent up pain and emotions she had kept hidden all those years were suddenly unleashed. Her screams were loud and heart rendering, but to the attackers frightening. She was vaguely aware of someone banging on the door, of voices shouting, people crowding in around her, some talking in a language she didn't understand. Only when she collapsed into the arms of Mario, did she feel safe. Sobbing quietly, she was carried through to his bench and there he held her gently till her sobs subsided.

Maria had always felt safe somehow with Mario. He had a calming effect on her. She used to imagine what it would be like to have a father like him. Kind and loving, in a very gentle and protective way. He was a very private person, no-one really knew anything about him. The whispers were that he was illegal and shouldn't be in the country. He was from the Ukraine. Maria had heard them talking about him often, but on-one would say anything to his face. They were afraid of him. He stood over six feet tall, with a very hard muscular body and eyes that threatened anyone who looked at him.

It was only as he calmed Maria down, stroked her hair and kissed away her tears, he admitted he had once had a daughter just like her; she had looked exactly like her mother. He stopped talking to wipe his own tears away then smiled.

"But that is just between us" he said.

Maria clung to him. At last there was some-one who cared, and wanted nothing from her, she wished she could stay there with his arm around her forever, feeling safe and protected.

The following day, one of the ladies came down from the office and asked Maria to go with her. At first Maria thought she was in trouble and would have to finish work, but it wasn't so. Mario had asked the lady to explain some of the facts of life to her, to help her understand the ways of men and how she should react and not be afraid but to welcome womanhood and the changes her body was experiencing.

Maria was so glad for that day, because her body had changed and Maria now knew there was nothing wrong with her, her body was just preparing itself for motherhood. But with that knowledge came a determination that she would never have children and definitely wasn't going to have a man. After all, look what it did to her ma. She had never known a day's happiness since she had met her father. At least that's what she said. "And look at me" she thought bitterly, "I loved you David, more than anyone else ever will, yet you left me. You betrayed me in the worst way anyone could. I'll never forget you. Because you will always remind me of what happens when you love someone." Maria paused as tears filled her eyes. "I will never love again," she whispered hoarsely, "Never". Yet inside she knew she would always love David, she couldn't help it.

"The hopelessness of life overshadows the realities of what really is and will always be." It was a passage she had read in a book long ago and never really understood it. But then she had been full of hope and ambition, her only goal was to look after her family and save until she could take them home. How simple life had been then, she thought. How uncomplicated and straightforward everything was. At that time she had no feeling for anyone except her family. Life had been so clear-cut, whereas now it seemed complicated, fuzzy, with too many emotions filling her head, bringing confusion, making her feel as though she were no longer in control and she didn't like it. It was as if she had lost her direction in life and was going the wrong way. She hated these thoughts. She wanted to feel as though she were doing the right thing, but the realities escaped her. She was floundering and couldn't understand why.

Maria felt trapped. Her mother would never get better, her life couldn't improve without David, and so, no matter how hard she tried, everything she did seemed meaningless. She felt as though her life was one long round of misery with only the pain of loneliness for company.

"I have lost everything in life," she sobbed, and the tears fell so forlornly she looked like a small broken doll with no one to love her. All the feelings she had ever held dear had come crushing down like a series of events that yielded an unending path of tragic sorrow cascading around her. She started to think maybe she was like her mother, not knowing reality when it presented itself. This thought quickly left her and she knew she could never be like her mother, not even for an instant. Yes, her heart was broken. Her mind not functioning as it should, but all she could think of was David and his new bride. It wasn't fair! Life wasn't fair! But who said it was? As long as she could remember it had never been fair.

In the following weeks Maria went through the mechanics of life like a robot. Work, school, family all took her time, but nothing could fix her heart. She never heard from David. But that never stopped her from hoping, and every day she would wait for the letter. But it never came.

It was one day when she was working beside Mario, who was so nice to be near, that Maria could feel herself losing control of her emotions. She desperately needed a friend.

When he turned and looked deeply into her eyes, asked her to smile, she just broke down and cried and all the pain and heartache she felt came pouring out. He listened quietly, until she was spent and exhausted.

"Your young life has not prepared you for an emotion as strong as love," he said. "But think, understand, you know little of David's life. He has suffered more than you will ever comprehend because you have to live it to feel it. David is trying to repay a little of what was given to him, but more than that, he had a life once, a family. So if he can help make one person happy who has gone through what he has gone through, then he will feel he has achieved one small thing to give back to humanity, to the race he belongs to, to the people he loves and owes so much, too much. So, my little Maria, accept David may love you, but will never be in a position to commit to you. That's not to say his heart isn't breaking as yours is. And I really think it is."

"Do you really mean that Mario?"

"Yes, we all have memories and commitments we can't talk about, so accept the friendship he offers. It's all he can give. And believe me, friendship can sometimes mean more than anything if it's given in love."

"I have been selfish haven't I?"

"No, you are still a child, but I suspect you have never known childhood. The grown up world is very complex, but" he smiled, "you are doing very well."

She wiped the tears from her eyes, "Thank you," she whispered.

Then came the words she didn't want to hear. "Maria, I am so sorry, but I have to tell you I to will be leaving soon, I have no choice."

She felt suddenly terribly lost and lonely. A sadness so great overwhelmed her, as she realised she didn't have a friend in the world.

Chapter Thirteen.

Without Mario she no longer felt safe working there but what choice did she have? Inside she was filled with a coldness she couldn't explain, an emptiness that wouldn't go away and an ambition that didn't seem to give her the push like it used to. She felt weak and useless for the first time in her life. She no longer had the strength to fight, she couldn't cope. There was no one left to talk to, she was so overcome with loneliness she didn't know what to do.

She arrived home after a hard day, tired and hungry, wanting only to slip into bed after she had eaten some of the soup she'd made the night before. But Tim was waiting for her.

"Maria, there's a job going on a market stall. You'll love it." He said enthusiastically.

Tim lived in the room upstairs with his wife Laura and baby Paul. They had come from the country. Tim was a young man in his early twenties, tall and slim with a mop of red hair and deep set green eyes. A pleasant man, always ready to help and give a smile. His Laura, as he referred to her tenderly, was also disposed of a kind and gentle nature. Maria often used to wonder why they were so happy as they were so poor. She could hear them pleading for more time to pay the rent when Ada came round on a Thursday night

"I don't think so Tim, but thanks anyway."

"Give it a try Maria, you've nothing to lose." he insisted.

As she looked into his eyes, his open honest eyes she realised he was right. She didn't have anything to lose, she hated the job she had, it was poor wages and Mario had gone. Maybe it was time for a change.

"O.K. I'll give it a go "she said.

"You won't be sorry, honest"

"I haven't got the job yet Tim"

"No but I have a good feeling about it"

Maria smiled, she remembered when she used to have good feelings about things, but that seemed so long ago.

The following day, Tim took Maria round to the shop window where he had read the advert and there it was in black and white. Large bold writing which stood out from the crisp whiteness of the paper which drew your eyes to it instantly. 'High class market stall, selling the best in fashionable knitwear, has a part time vacancy for a smart well-spoken young lady'. It was for Saturdays only to begin with and seemed well paid. It also offered full training.

Maria read it again before breaking out into a wide smile.

"That's me, a well-spoken young lady," she said.

"Well what do you think?

"I think the job was made for me" she said pulling his arm. "Let's go"

"The owner is probably a big scruffy old man," she said, "knowing my luck".

Together they made their way along Bury New Road towards the market. It was a dark day with overcast clouds and a permanent light rain, the kind of rain you weren't really aware of but which soaked you to the skin anyway. Maria was totally unaware of everything around her and had only the prospect of a new job on her mind. At last she felt as though something good was about to happen. This job was outdoors and that really appealed to her. The factory had been so dark and dismal with no natural daylight coming in; she had found it depressing sometimes. Also, everyone was so busy there, with very little conversation between the workers. Your wages depended on the quantity of work you produced. So everyone just concentrated on doing as much as they could, like her, earning money was all they cared about. But this was different.

At last they arrived. Tim stood on the corner as Maria went over to the stall to ask about the job. It was a nice stall, clean and attractive, gaily coloured clothes hung around the makeshift walls and the counter was piled high with neatly folded woollen garments. It looked a very well organised stall and that was always a good sign.

As Tim watched, Maria appeared to be laughing; the young man with her was obviously impressed. Tim crossed his fingers; hoping it was going as well as it looked. He knew she needed this job more than she realised. To be out in the fresh air talking to people was more in line with her character than being stuck in a factory. And Tim was the one who would know this as he too, had, had to work in a factory before getting work on the market. Even now after only a few weeks, he felt as though he had been doing it for years, he was so happy working with people in an open environment enjoying the relaxed banter with the public. He knew he could never do anything else.

Maria looked radiant; she was smiling from ear to ear.

"I just can't believe it Tim," she said breathlessly as she returned. "He never even asked me how old I was or anything. He just said I would be perfect for the job and can I start on Saturday. I will be working in Salford, wherever that is?"

"It's not far, you'll love it. It's like a different world, the people are really great."

"What do you mean 'it's like a different world'?"

"It just is. Wait till you go, then you'll know what I mean."

Maria eyed him suspiciously.

"It's brilliant you got the job, and I know you will just love it, honest. Have I ever been wrong?"

"You know what Tim,"

"What?"

"There is always a first time but I have to admit that was one of your better ideas" she laughed happily. Her eyes sparkled and her whole body seemed to come alive. `Maybe, just maybe` she thought, life was going to be good to her.

It was as Tim said, she was happy. She loved her work and Michael the owner never asked her to work during the week. So her age and the fact she was at school was never an issue.

Maria was completely captivated by Michael. He definitely wasn't old and ugly as she once thought he might be. He was gorgeous. And every time she looked at him, her heart would beat that little bit faster. He felt the same, she could tell. It was in his eyes, they came alive when he looked at her. She was so happy. She was fourteen and in love. Michael was a lot older than her but still a young man. Anyway, she didn't care. It had been an instant attraction. They looked like each other, both dark, both bright eyed with large personalities and even larger ambitions. It was a partnership made in heaven.

With Maria's help it soon progressed to two stalls. She was a natural; a born sales person with a quick brain and a mind that could add up instantly. It was 1955, the school was closed for the summer holidays and Maria found herself being with Michael for most of the time. He soon realised what an asset she was. She took more in sales than he had ever done. In fact she took more in one day than he took in two. He needed her, but he also enjoyed being with her, she was fun. He knew she was infatuated with him and took full advantage of it. Having a beautiful young girl looking up to him, made him feel good, in fact he couldn't have wished for more. Oh he knew she was young, but he wasn't about to tell her that he knew, it would spoil his plans.

Michael smiled to himself. The excuse he had given his family for hiring her was the truth. She was a schoolgirl, this had been confirmed by his friend, but instead of putting him off, he found it exciting. It was exactly what he wanted and needed, a fresh young beautiful girl, full of innocence. He couldn't believe his luck. And what a powerful argument it would make when the time came for him to declare his love.

"Yes" he smiled to himself feeling smug, "Life is good."

Michael's family seemed to accept everything he did. He

did seem to have a tendency for young girls, but as his father said, "It was good for business, and there was no harm in it."

Michael on the other hand used to say, in all innocence. "I didn't know she was so young when I employed her, but she is a very good worker."

The business he was so proud of was in fact his father's, but he omitted to tell anyone that. He lived in his own private little dream world, which his parents closed their eyes to.

Maria loved her work, she loved the people and the outdoors, and most especially she loved the fact that poverty never seemed to be a problem to them. The women would laugh and sing even in the street. The children played happily though most had hardly any clothes on. These people in Salford never ceased to amaze her. They loved life. It was as if everything was perfect. Elvis Presley was in the charts and his songs could be heard on almost everyone's lips, along with the quick remarks and innuendoes as they crooned along with the words. It was a different world, and Maria loved every minute of it.

After a time, Michael, who had carefully courted her without her realising it, began to make her dependent on his emotions. She thought it would never happen again but she felt happy. It wasn't the kind of feeling she felt for David, but she convinced herself it was love. He was what she needed to help her get through life, to make some kind of sense of all the pain she felt. And, she smiled he was kind of gorgeous looking with sparkling eyes and a happy smile."

"Do you mind if I talk to you Maria?"

"Why should I mind?"

"Then tell me, why do you cry over something you can't have"?

"I don't know what you mean."

"Oh come on Maria, everyone knows you have the hots for that David."

"Yeh, well everyone's wrong" Maria turned her back to hide the tears that were threatening to escape.

"I don't want you, or anyone else talking about me," she answered gaining control of her emotions. She turned to face him, her eyes cold and expressionless.

"You don't understand anything."

"Course I do. He professes everlasting love, you believe him, then he goes off and marries someone else."

"Stop it, it's not like that, he's good, kind and decent. Just leave me alone will you."

"Okay, I'm sorry, maybe I was talking out of turn. I didn't mean to upset you. Tell you what, just to prove how much I like and respect you, you can come out with us tonight."

"Where are you going? Maria's emotions were in a mess. She had gone from happiness to abject misery, she couldn't help it. No matter what she told herself, she knew David would always be there. He was the one she desperately needed. But it was making her feel so unhappy.

"Hey, cheer up I didn't mean to upset you that much."

She smiled wanly, "You still haven't told me where you are going."

"Me and the gang, we meet up after we finish on a Saturday and go for a drink and a chat. You know, talk about how work is going, and what's new in the fashion world and what we can copy." He smiled broadly at his last remark.

Maria felt elated; the idea of going out with them was absolutely fantastic. But her mind was in a turmoil, he obviously didn't know how old she was, or he wouldn't have asked her to go to the pub. Should she tell him? She really didn't know. What if she went and they wouldn't serve her? What would she do if they asked her to leave? She would feel absolutely mortified. But then, if she went and was accepted, they would treat her as an adult and an equal and that's what she wanted more than ever in life.

The decision was made! She would take a chance, she wanted to belong, to be treated as an adult and this was her chance.

It was nothing like she expected. The pub was warm and comfortable, the seats were beautifully upholstered and the floor was covered in carpet. Soft music played in the back ground. Pictures adorned the walls, Maria was in shock. She was so overwhelmed by the sheer exuberance of the place. It was like stepping into another world. A world where there was no poverty or dirt.

"No wonder people came to pubs, it's better than being at home," she whispered quietly in awe.

Michael smiled as he sat her down in front of a large open fire, before going to the bar for the drinks. Thankfully he never asked Maria what she wanted. She was dreading it because she had never tasted alcohol before and wouldn't know what to say. Underneath she was hoping he would buy her a soft drink as distant memories of her father came flooding back. She remembered what he had been like, and how her mother used to cry, calling it the demon drink. Suddenly she was quite afraid, having no knowledge of drink she felt out of her depth as old memories started to haunt her. Just as she was about to take flight, Michael appeared all smiling and happy. Maria chastised herself, she was over reacting and her imagination was running wild. It was just the memory of her father.

"Why now?" She couldn't understand it. She hadn't thought about him for a while. But he never ceased to make her angry. Tonight though, she wasn't going to let anything spoil her night. She smiled up at Michael, studying his face. He really was so handsome she couldn't believe she was actually sitting there in a pub with him.

"For you my lady, a Cherry B complete with its own cherry on top"

he said bowing, handing her a dainty glass.

"Oh Michael, stop it you're embarrassing me" she said looking around her to see if anybody was watching. But to her complete surprise no one seemed to notice, they all seemed to be locked into their own little world, chatting quietly to each other.

"Will it make me drunk?" she said taking the glass from him.

"No my cherub, I have it on good authority it's made from cherries, hence the name, it's all healthy and full of goodness."

Holding the glass gently, she removed the cherry and savoured every little bit as she ate it slowly, it tasted absolutely wonderful. Maria felt so grown up, only that morning Michael had given her a beautiful deep red floral dress, it was the latest fashion with full skirt and fitted bodice. At first she had felt self-conscious, but after having received many compliments throughout the day, she admitted Michael was right. To sell clothes you had to wear them and look good. She had drawn her hair back into a pony tail and held it together with a matching scarf. Across her shoulders draped a cream coloured cardigan interwoven with a deep burgundy thread. To finish off the look, he gave her a gold waspi belt which fitted snugly around her waist, emphasizing the fullness of her curves.

She felt good, very good, and as she sipped her drink she couldn't help but think how lucky she was that Tim had recommended she go for this job. Maria started to relax, a warm feeling was spreading through her body. She was happy the others couldn't make it, she wanted this night to stay just as it was.

After her second drink Maria started to feel strange.

"It's because you're hungry. Look I don't mind, I live just round the corner, and as luck would have it my mother always makes more than enough food"

"Won't she mind?"

"Of course not, in fact she's always telling me to bring a nice girl home."

Maria smiled, trying to clear her head a little. She didn't really want another drink but then she didn't want to look ungrateful either.

Michael's mother was out, but by this time Maria was no longer in full control of her actions, she just wanted to lie down. Michael held her and whispered all the right things to make her feel better. He placed her on the bed, helped her out of the new clothes just in case she creased them, and then told her to relax and have a little sleep.

Gratefully she closed her eyes, never had she felt like this before, it was like living in a dream world. Vaguely she was aware of someone next to her, of hands gentle caressing her body, making her feel all warm and relaxed and yet there was something else she was feeling. Something so good she wanted it to go on and on, she was aware of being held, of feeling arms around her, somewhere in the back of her mind something was telling her she was naked, but she no longer cared. She could only hear the words she had waited her whole life to hear, she clung to him as he whispered over and over again.

"I love you Maria, I love you." And as he whispered quietly to her, his hands explored, and his kisses swept over her softly, passionately, yet tenderly. Their bodies became entwined as one. He aroused her as she had never been aroused; he made her feel a passion so strong it overtook everything her young mind might be trying to tell her.

He stroked her hair, kissed her lips, whispered wonderful things and all the time he was drawing on her innocence, making her feel the strength of her emotions, encouraging her to let go, to give in, to fill the need her body was aching for. And as her need rose he waited, waited until she could no longer wait, then as her passion built almost to the point of no return, he entered her. Her lips parted but no words came out, nothing could have prepared her for this. Locked together moving passionately as one, her body rising to his, there was no going back. He could feel the warmth of her body taking him, felt her need, her passion, and yes her pain as he whispered words of love. Tears ran from her eyes as the power of pure pleasure engulfed her, and when she couldn't take anymore she lay spent and exhausted. The alcohol dimming her mind she slept happily in the arms of the man who loved her.

Sometime later she awoke to find she was alone, he had left a note.

"Sorry, had to go out. Be careful going home. See you at work tomorrow.

Michael. P.S. I love you."

Maria smiled, he loved her and that was all that mattered. Now she felt like a woman. Now she felt strong and confident and there was nothing she couldn't do. Life had at last, taken on a new meaning.

Chapter Fourteen.

Was it really only ten o'clock, Maria stopped and looked at her reflection in the shop window. She seemed the same, she reasoned, and yet in just a few hours she had gone from a lovesick child to a fully-fledged woman in love. But more importantly she was loved back, and for the first time in her young life, Maria felt as though she belonged. That night Maria slept fitfully. One minute she was happy, thinking about Michael, remembering how his arms felt wrapped around her, hearing his words of love. Then an overwhelming feeling of despair would engulf her.

In her dream, David seemed to be watching her from a distance, like he was on the other side of the road, he was there, then he wasn't, but his eyes rested on hers, they were sad. She thought he was trying to tell her something but the words wouldn't come out. Over and over the same dream disturbed her until eventually she awoke. Tired and confused she went about her daily tasks ignoring her mother's looks and the never-ending questions from John.

"Why were you late?" he asked, "we were looking for you. You never come home late."

"John, I am a lot older than you, I can stay out if I want to."

"You're not that much older," he stated boldly. Maria looked at him, he was right, she was fourteen, and he was twelve. But there was a lifetime's difference between them.

"I was so scared" he said simply, "what would we do without you?

Maria felt guilty when she saw the sadness in his eyes. He was right. They did live on a very delicate line, and yes, they were all vulnerable. Worse than that, she had allowed her own feelings to forget momentarily her promise to them. John had brought her down to earth. He had made her realise that if she was ever to get her own life together then she would have to take them home to Scotland. But then what? She was still too young to be on her own. She wasn't even old enough to leave school. As far as she was concerned, she was a woman in love, was feeling like a woman, but the law said, she was a child. She had to think, she had to have some kind of plan. Maria hated uncertainty. Everything had to be planed and organised, that was her nature.

"Good morning" Michael smiled, as she arrived at work. Then he pulled her behind the curtain, kissed her full on the lips, bringing all kinds of emotions to the fore.

She loved being with him, he made her forget all her problems, and while she was with him, felt as if the rest of the world didn't exist. Maria realised there was nothing she could do about taking them back to Scotland just yet. One, she didn't have enough money and two, she wanted to wait until she had left school. And that wouldn't be until she was fifteen years old.

Her main fear at the moment was telling Michael the truth. Soon the summer holidays would be over, and she would have to return to school. Half of her was frightened of losing him but the other half thought he loved her too much, to let age get in the way. When the time came though, she was terrified of losing him. She needed him more than anything in her life. All her problems at home paled as her happiness at being with him filled every waking moment. Only in sleep did she have regrets, and she put that down to the fact their relationship was still a secret.

And so, on one wet Saturday afternoon, as the rain poured down and they were huddled together behind the stall, Maria told him. At first, he pretended to be angry and said he was going to end it there and then. She was devastated. Then he gently put his arms around her and with a very convincing lie, made her believe he couldn't live without her.

"It is against the law." he said, "but I love you so much, I'm willing to take the chance. I know I could be sent to prison, but I love you too much to be separated from you."

"You would do that for me; take a chance on being sent to prison?"

"Yes my love, I would."

"Oh Michael, you are so good to me."

"And when you are fifteen, we will tell the world." He stated proudly.

With her head on his shoulder, the rain dripping down, his arm around her, Maria had never been happier.

The following day, Ada waited patiently to speak to Maria. It was something she felt she had to do.

"What is it Ada?"

"I just think you are too young, you are going to be hurt."

"He will never hurt me, he loves me."

"How do you know?"

"Oh Ada, I can feel it. I have never in my whole life felt so happy. Michael said that when I'm fifteen he'll take me home to meet his family."

"That, to me, is a very flimsy excuse not to be responsible, or to commit him." Ada said, obviously worried.

"I won't let you talk to me like that. We love each other and we're going to get married."

"Did he say that?"

Maria went quiet. She knew he had never really said that. But he did say over and over again how much he loved her, and surely that meant the same.

"Maria," Ada said softly, "some boys, or should I say men, say things like that when they want more than they should have, without marriage."

"Ada, what we have will last. He loves me. We belong to each other."

Chapter Fifteen.

Ada knew there was now no turning back for Maria. She had grown up before her time, but this was something she had no experience of. Men were not to be trusted. Ada prayed to God that she was wrong, she didn't like Michael, and certainly didn't trust him. But she knew that at this moment Maria lived for him, without him she knew Maria would crumble. Deep down, Ada knew Maria still hurt over David. If Michael rejected Maria, Ada didn't know what would happen. Maria was just too young for this kind of thing, she couldn't bring herself to say love.

She wanted to grab Michael, tell him to find someone his own age, to leave her alone. But Ada knew that would not solve anything, she could only hope it would run its course.

"Please Lord," she prayed, "no babies; let her grow up away from him. Let her be free to enjoy her life. She's suffered too much."

Then, holding her head in her hands, she cried, she felt so much for this child who desperately wanted to be a woman.

Maria was spending as much time as she could with Michael and Ada had to admit they did seem good together. Their feelings seemed to have settled down into a more stable relationship. Maria blossomed, gone was the child and in its place was a very lovely young woman who seemed to know what she wanted. The only pain in her life, was the fact Michael hadn't taken her to meet his parents yet. She had originally agreed to wait until her birthday and as that was now approaching, she expected to be introduced. But then Michael told her he'd been mistaken and it was in fact sixteen before you could have a relationship like theirs. And, as he pointed out, he didn't want anyone to upset her or look down on her. He convinced her that if their love was to survive and be part of the love of his family, she would have to be patient. After all, they had their whole lives in front of them, why jeopardise the happiness they had by antagonising the family? Or, worse still, being sent to prison for a long time.

Maria had cried that day, heart-rending cries. She didn't understand life. But after a long restless sleep, she decided to accept that what she had at that moment was good. She didn't want to lose it. She didn't want it to change. Why take the chance of spoiling their happiness just because she wanted to be accepted by his family. Michael was right, there was no rush, they knew, they loved each other. In time, when it was the right thing to do, they would tell the world.

Meanwhile, they worked hard, and one afternoon a week they checked into a small hotel and spent the most wonderful hours making love and simply being happy.

Maria would dream they could stay there forever. Michael promised that when the time came, he would make her the happiest woman in the world. Nothing would be too good for her, and they would be free to love openly and let everyone who had doubted their love (meaning Ada) would accept and see that they belonged together.

It was as her life was beginning to be settled and she felt almost contented. Christmas had just gone and for the first time they had been together as a family and opened presents. They were happy. It was January 1956 and Maria had celebrated her 15th birthday, she couldn't wait for Easter to come as that was the next term when she could leave school. And then she would be able to spend every day with Michael. But then Ada delivered the blow that was to bring her back to reality...

"Your Ma is sick Maria, she's getting worse and I fear for her life."

"What do you mean Ada?"

"I mean she's dying."

"She can't be! You said yourself she was sick in the head not the body."

"Yes, but she has given up, her life is wasting away. Look at her, see how she has changed. Maria I mean it, take her home or lose her."

Maria sat down in shock. It was true she hadn't given her mother much thought lately, but that's not because she didn't care. She had just become used to her always being in bed, living in her own world. It never entered her head that her ma could die. Her mother had just become someone who lived in bed and didn't really care about anything. Maria felt devastated and guilty.

"You're right Ada. I didn't know. I'm sorry. We will take her home. It's what she has always wanted. I'll make all the arrangements, but first I want to see Michael, I want to be the one to tell him I have to go."

It was one of the hardest things she had ever done, telling Michael she was going away and didn't know for how long.

"It is for the best Maria, if you don't go and something happens to your ma you will never forgive yourself."

"Yes I know."

"But?"

"But I don't want to go, I love you, I can't bear the thought of being without you."

"You have to go, take them home, I will be waiting for you. Because, my darling, it's the right thing to do and we have eternity to be together." He smiled.

Maria sank into his arms, wanting to believe him. She knew she had to go, she knew it was the right thing, so why did she feel something was wrong. There was a tightening of her stomach muscles and a quickening of the heart. Michael had said everything she had wanted to hear, but somehow something wasn't quite right. What it was, she didn't know. Maybe her mind was playing tricks, she thought, but she knew that wasn't the truth. She had lived her life listening to her feelings, only now at this moment as she looked at Michael did she want to dismiss them.

The following days passed in a flurry of activity as they prepared to leave and go to this magical place called home. Gone was the quiet sullen person who never spoke, in its place was a very childlike woman who chattered incessantly about her childhood, her parents and the place where she grew up. She blossomed in front of them, but only Maria realised her mother's life didn't include them. It started and finished with herself. Maybe, Maria thought, her grandparents would welcome them all home and her mother would come to realise it was alright for her to love her children.

For a few fleeting moments Maria pictured them all in the big house as her mother had described it. They were all happy and even Michael would come up and visit. And when she was old enough they would give her a most wonderful wedding and invite everyone. They would be so proud of her. But she knew that would never happen. It was just a dream. Meanwhile she had sent her grandparents a letter giving them no choice but to accept the fact their daughter was coming home and she was sick.

Now at the thought of going to the place they all called home, Maria was apprehensive. Home, something her mother had always referred to when talking about her childhood. She said it was the only place in the whole world that was home. And that's how they had all come to think of it. Except Maria would never forget that first letter that said they weren't wanted and never to return. At the time she had vowed she would never go and sworn she would never want meet them. But now she had no choice, she was taking them home because she had to. She had to make her Ma well.

"Will it be like a palace?" John asked Maria.

"Not quite, but I think it will be big, very big." she smiled,

"But they do have a cook don't they Maria, and someone who cleans the house for them? They do, don't they?"

"Yes I believe so."

"Then we won't have anything to do will we?"

Maria loved John. He was so open, so trusting and gave his love freely. Cathy on the other hand, she was sorry to say, was like her mother. No-one ever knew what she was thinking or feeling. She was locked into her own private world where anything was possible but rarely happened. Maria just hoped Cathy would never get sick in the head like mother, and that once she got home would be happy.

Maria knew it was not normal for one as young as Cathy to be permanently miserable. She blamed her mother, but then on hindsight she realised the blame still sat squarely at her father's door. To cheer everyone up, Maria said she was taking them all shopping into Manchester for new clothes. After all, when they arrived home they didn't want to look poor, they would be clean and well dressed and their grandparents would be proud of them. And mother can show us off to everyone, and let them see what a wonderful family we are.

Everyone jumped for joy, even her mother seemed happy at going shopping, something she had always refused to do. Suddenly everything changed, they were all laughing and chatty and giggly, they had never been so happy.

If only it was like this all the time, Maria thought, still unsure of what kind of welcome they would get, though to be truthful she knew Cathy and John would be alright. It was herself she didn't want to think about. All her life she had only heard how everything bad that had happened to everyone had been her fault. And that she didn't belong.

The day was finally here, they were all packed and ready to go. Maria looked at herself in the mirror. Her hair was tied back in a ponytail emphasising her well-structured face. She was happy as her fingers felt the soft wool of the figure hugging sweater which was tucked into a full flared skirt with lots of pretty petticoats underneath. Her waist was naturally tiny but the little leather belt with its silver buckle accentuated just how tiny it was, giving her the perfect hour glass figure. But it was her shoes she really liked. She had decided to treat herself to a modern pair of small high heels, 'Baby Louise' the young lady who was serving them had said they were called. The high heeled court shoes had looked more sophisticated, but then she pictured herself toppling over. She remembered laughing in the shop and the assistant looking at her strangely, but she didn't care, nothing could dampen her spirit, except Michael. For some unknown reason he still didn't seem right, even though he had never said anything wrong or out of place. On the contrary, he professed everlasting love on every occasion, so why was she so worried?

She wasn't due to see Michael until tomorrow, but Tim came down to see her and suggested a walk. He was agitated, she knew something was wrong. It would have to be serious she thought because Tim was one of life's optimists, he was so laid back nothing seemed to bother him.

"O.K. what's wrong?" she finally asked.

"I don't know how to tell you, or even if I should, it's only a rumour"

"You can't stop now," she said. "Spit it out."

Although she wanted to know, Maria had a cold feeling in her stomach. She knew whatever it was it had to do with her, and it would be the truth.

"Tell me Tim"

"I am so sorry Maria."

"Tim" she said in exasperation and fear.

"It's Michael, he has hired someone else."

"Is that all? I'm taking everyone back to Scotland, I would

expect him to."

"No, you don't understand, apparently she's young."

"So?"

"So everyone was talking, said it was time. Michael only likes kids and when they get old he finds somebody young again."

Tim went quiet. He wouldn't hurt Maria for anything but he couldn't allow her to find out from anyone else.

Maria stared at him as the words penetrated her brain.

"Take me to the stall." she whispered.

"No please don't." he begged.

"I have to."

Silently they walked together, Maria smiled.

"It's raining," she said. "It always seems to be raining."

Maria stopped; it was on the same corner Tim had stood when she was being interviewed. They had been so happy that day. It gave Maria a good clear view of the stall. Shock washed over her as she stood rooted to the spot, watching Michael do everything she remembered so vividly, the smile, the touches, and the intimacy before he made his move. She bitterly realised what he was really like. The girl was young, obviously still at school and with that dreamy expression of naivety and love.

"Was that me?" she thought "not so very long ago."

Michael looked as he always looked, handsome, relaxed, and smiling. And then it hit her. He was so like her father! Why hadn't she noticed the resemblance before? He looked like him, acted like him, and certainly chased the women like him. Only Michael didn't chase women did he? He courted innocent young girls who knew no better.

As Maria stood there she filled with a deep loathing of her own weakness. He had hurt her. She had loved him and had trusted him. Now the rage she felt inside was at breaking point. She was tired of always being the one that got hurt. It was time for her to do the hurting.

"Are you alright?" Tim asked studying her face.

"Yes" she said simply, turning to him. "I made a mistake, it won't happen again."

She spoke quietly with a strength he had never heard "And," she added with conviction, "I am going to be rich, very rich."

Then, as she walked away she once again felt the cold determination to succeed, and knew the real truth of life. Love like thorns, only brought pain.

Chapter Sixteen.

From the outside it was an unimpressive building. It was large, ugly, and had no character. Opening her purse, she double-checked the name and address, and couldn't help but smile. She was actually smiling at her own stupidity.

"How on earth, did I fall for such a low life" she asked herself, thinking of Michael. Even his business was a lie, his father owned it, and from what she had heard, he was worse than his son.

"Oh well," she said, "here goes."

She entered the building with the step of a very confident young woman, though she felt anything but. "Still," she thought "I have nothing to lose and lots to gain, especially when it comes to hopefully putting him in his place." Holding her head high she asked in a clear voice to see Mr Pervare.

"I'm sorry he's not seeing anyone today," replied a very timid looking receptionist dressed in black.

"She must be at least 60 years old" Maria thought, "and very plain." She couldn't help but stare at the woman, she had dark steely grey hair tied back in a very unattractive dull clasp which didn't quite do the job properly.

"I said, you can't see him today" the woman repeated.

Maria realised she had been staring as the woman was obviously uncomfortable.

"Yes I did hear you," she replied, "but I have come to see him and nothing is going to stop me."

The woman paled, unused to being spoken to like that and, lifting the receiver, dialled her boss in the next room.

Maria could hear him shouting at the poor woman, this made her feel all the more determined. Going over to the door she knocked loudly before entering.

"And just what do you think you are doing coming in here, demanding to see me?"

"If knocking on your door is demanding I obviously don't know the true meaning of the word."

"Look young lady I don't want to see you. I know who you are, leave my son alone or I'll get the police."

"Good, I would like that." Maria said defiantly looking up into the face of Michael's father. He was tall, large, bordering on fat, with droopy eyes and thick lips that looked like they had never known how to smile. His skin was sallow, sickly looking, Maria couldn't help it. She smiled as she stared at him. She thought if Michael had taken her home to meet the family, she would probably have run a mile. There was nothing remotely nice about his father, nor on reflection, had there been about Michael.

"What do you find amusing? Are you stupid or something? I said I was going to phone the police."

"Good, phone them."

"O.K. what is your problem?"

"I don't have one, you have, his name is Michael."

"My son isn't a problem, he just has poor taste in women. Now get out."

He opened the door wide, shouting to a young lad to escort her from the building.

Maria looked round, no-one intimidated her anymore. She was what she was, and that was better than anyone here. A young boy appeared at the door. She watched him looking nervously at his employer, who was going redder in the face by the moment. It was clear he wasn't used to being spoken to like that, especially by a woman. He had made that quite clear. Maria, on the other hand, didn't care what he thought. She realised that, with the amount of staff he had and the size of his warehouse, this was no ordinary little business with a couple of market stalls.

She turned to face him square on and pulling herself up; she stood as tall and as straight as she could then pushed past him, walking further into his office. He was furious.

"How dare you"

But before he could say anymore she interrupted him.

"I am a minor," she said icily.

"And," he bellowed.

"Your son got me drunk, then raped me."

At that moment the young man gasped

Mr. Pervare turned to the door, he had momentary forgotten the boy was there.

"You wanted me Mr Pervare?"

He stood not knowing what to do; throw her out, or listen to her. He looked from one to the other, she wasn't backing down.

"Come back in five minutes," he growled.

"Even if it's true what you say, and I don't think for one moment it is, what's that got to do with me? If you are trying to blackmail me, I won't have it, I don't believe you, you are nothing but......

"Shut up, I am nothing but a kid who is sick of people like you who take and use people for their own corrupt way. Your son is sick in the head if he thinks he can get away with it and you are more stupid than I thought if you agree with him."

Mr Pervare's temper was at exploding point; he raised his hand about to lose control.

"Go on hit me, I'm sure that will look good next to the rape charge." Maria stood her ground her face set in stony indifference, her eyes cold.

He sank into his chair; he had used bullying, shouting, intimidation. It had all worked in the past. His son just couldn't keep away from schoolgirls, but this time he had picked the wrong one. He realised he had a problem. This one was not going to go away.

"O.K.," he said sounding resigned. "What do you want?"

"I want a double stall in Salford, a trader's licence and enough money to fully stock them for one month and wages for two staff for a month."

"You are too young."

"That's my problem, I will supply the paper work, you supply the money."

"And if I don't?"

"I go to the police, your son goes to prison and I'll make sure your reputation goes to the dogs. Oh, and by the way, I know one or two of your cheap labour lads, they are illegal. So all in all I think you are getting off lightly. After all, how many girls has your son hurt, and how often have you covered up?"

The sheer hate inside her could be felt in the air like a tangible presence. Mr Pervare had never felt like this before and definitely wouldn't have expected something like this from a slip of a girl. But then as he looked at her, with eyes as deep and as black as he had ever seen and hair that hung wildly and shone with the same deep dark colour as her eyes, he shivered. Back home they had a name for people like her, she was possessed.

Maria saw the fleeting look of fear in his eyes, and knew she had won. She didn't know what or why he had experienced fear, but she knew she was going to use it. And she also knew that it would have to be a little bit longer before she took her ma and the children back home.

Chapter Seventeen.

Adrenalin soared through Maria's body as she ran upstairs to Tim shouting for John and Cathy to follow.

"What's up. Sis?" This was the latest craze from John. It was the 50s, with D.A. haircuts, strange styles of clothing and lots of language short cuts.

"We're going to have a market stall of our own, a double one in Salford." she said excitedly.

"How? When?" Tim said, "What about the money?"

"First we want a name." she said, ignoring his question.

"You'll have to be the one who signs for the licence to trade, Tim as I'm too young."

"No problem, but we need a name."

"Well, we are Tim and Maria, how about Timar?"

"Not really a fine knitwear name, as much as I like it."

"I know," Maria said. "What about Laura May?"

"Wow" Laura said, "that's my name."

"I think it's a very pretty name," Cathy said thoughtfully.

"You know Cathy; you just amaze me more each day,"

Maria said smiling at her.

"I agree with Cathy," Tim said. "It is pretty."

So, they were agreed, and Laura felt so proud, proud of the fact her name was being used but more so that her husband, her Tim, was going into business with Maria. She had always dreamt of them having a business but she thought it would take years and years, and now here they were, picking a name for one.

After all the excitement had calmed down Maria took hold of Cathy and John and explained that they were still going home, but they'd have to wait until she finished school. For though she had turned fifteen she still had to wait until the end of term, before she could get her leaving certificate. And, as she explained, it would give her too many problems to leave without it. However as luck would have it, the market stall would give them the opportunity to earn some extra money to take with them. It was a little white lie, but Maria felt it was the easiest way to break the news.

Over the next week, the contents of the stalls had been carefully picked. Maria had chatted up one of the warehouse boys she knew to pick up and deliver all her garments. She hoped she would sell most of them and they could manage to carry the rest back themselves. Maria knew they would make enough money for Tim to take driving lessons and so went ahead and organised some. Tim, for his part, had a friend who would let him practise and so knew he would get his licence quite soon.

Things were looking good. Maria never divulged where the money had come from and Tim never asked. At last, the day came. Tim, John, even Cathy, got up at five o'clock in the morning and together with Maria made their way to Salford

Market. There they met Ezekiel, who brought the goods Maria had ordered from the warehouse. She had a good eye and had studied what woollens were being worn and what colours were popular, but more importantly, she had noted what age group was doing the all the buying. It was a cold winter's day in February and Maria was so pleased she had taken a calculated risk in buying all warm wintry woollens in delicate pastels, and knew today would prove her right. It was cold but dry. Even Laura had walked up with young Paul who was now two and her new baby daughter Emma. Cathy had sat happily watching when Tim and John went for a hot drink, feeling very important. When the boys came back Maria had said it was the girls' turn to take a break from work. Cathy positively glowed with happiness at being called a worker. Maria was very contented, she felt as though she had at last arrived in that all too elusive place 'the grown up world'.

When she had stood back earlier in the morning and surveyed the stalls they had worked so hard at dressing, matching the colours, sizes and shapes, she had been filled a tremendous amount of pride and sense of achievement. But now, as they packed away what little was left, she truly felt successful. Each of them couldn't wait to see how much money they had made.

Sitting in Tim's room they laid out the money on the table while Laura served them tea. The aroma of a hot dinner coming from the kitchen was so appetizing they didn't know what to do first. They were very hungry, but they were also very excited.

"I think we should eat." Maria said, "money doesn't go cold."

After they had eaten and counted the money, they all relaxed happily and contented. It had been a huge success.

"Well, it doesn't stop here! We now have to work on our business plan." They all looked at Maria feeling a little tired, but they knew that with Maria there was no rest until she had everything under control.

"We need to know how we are to continue, pay our way and make us the most successful stall on the market. Agreed?"

"Agreed!" Everyone chirped.

"So let's write down what we need." Maria said, indicating some paper and a pen near to where Cathy sat.

"We have to always buy stock first, yes?"

They all nodded.

"And pay you a decent wage Tim, or Laura might stop feeding us." Maria laughed, but was also making the point that if she was out working all day, she didn't want to come home and start cooking. Laura, bless her, agreed whole heartedly and said that she was only too happy to help.

"I think then Tim, we need you to get your driving licence and buy a van. That way we can expand before next winter.

"My wages, you will be pleased to hear" she said, turning to John and Cathy, "are going to be put with yours until we have enough to take you both, and Ma back to Scotland." Cathy jumped up and kissed Maria, throwing her arms around her neck, John just smiled from ear to ear.

"When do you think that will be sis?"

"Hopefully in the summer holidays, when trade will slow a little and Tim can manage on his own. Then I'll be back to prepare for the winter trade." Maria looked at Tim for confirmation, for though she was confident everything would go to plan. She knew that without Tim and Laura she couldn't do it.

"Maria, you have given us a lifeline, a chance to make a life for ourselves, it's like a dream come true." He turned and smiled at his wife," It's something we have always wanted, isn't it Laura?"

Laura smiled happily, "We're right there with you Maria," she said. "You can count on us, that's a promise."

The following weeks far exceeded all their expectations of profit, Maria was a natural, but Tim also proved he was a born salesman. His easy manner, open, sincere face coupled with a good smile and personality, was a firm favourite with every one's mother as well as their daughters. Maria would smile as he effortlessly paired off colours with personalities and ages. He had the ability to make everyone feel special.

As well as her selling abilities, which she genuinely loved and knew she was good at, Maria excelled herself on the business side. She seemed to know instinctively what to buy, what to pay for it and to figure out a decent profit margin She also kept a keen eye on her competitors and what they sold, managing to undercut them wherever she could.

Life was beginning to feel good. They all worked well together. Occasionally she felt as though she was neglecting her mother. But Ada assured her she was alright; she made sure she had everything she needed. Ada had proved herself to be a gem, refusing any financial gain for looking after Ailsa and sometimes, when they were really busy, she would mind little Emma and Paul while Laura helped out on the stall.

As busy and as fulfilled she felt at the moment, Maria's confidence had risen tenfold as had her appearance. Whether it was because she was so confident or maybe it was the realisation she was doing what was right, both for her and her family, but she seemed to age overnight. She was still a very vibrant person, but gone was the naivety; she looked older than her years and could certainly put some of the older, more experienced traders in their place. Be it through tough negotiations, direct confrontations or plain old fashioned niceness. Maria always got what she wanted. She was happy, except on the rare occasions when she didn't collapse, exhausted into bed and she would remember David. He never wrote and that hurt. She still loved him and knew she always would. That little part of her heart was his, even if he never ever claimed it.

Business was booming, everything was going to plan. The money added up, Tim was lucky, he passed his driving test first time and that was through a cancellation so he hadn't had to wait too long. Michael had disappeared overnight, apparently he had moved to another site in Bolton. Tim and Maria soon earned the respect from the other traders. Also they managed to buy a cheap van from one of Tim's friends who was a mechanic. It made life so much easier, especially when they wanted to travel around Manchester and the surrounding areas to see what was being sold and what was being imported. The stalls were doing well but Maria wanted more.

"We have to think Tim, we have to expand. While I'm away, I'll concentrate" then she laughed, "While you can carry on making money!"

They had all slipped into a nice easy relationship with each other, even little Emma held up her arms to her when she saw her. Maria used Tim's room still to talk business because she didn't want her mother to listen to their plans, or know what they were doing.

Something inside her told her to hide it from her, she didn't trust her mother. She loved her but didn't trust her. The time was drawing near for Maria to take them all home. She had picked up four medium sized suitcases, one for each of them.

"You can fill it with what you like because we are all carrying our own, even mother." she said looking at her.

"Where are we going? I don't want to go anywhere, I'm sick I want to stay here."

On and on she groaned, until Maria, exercising great control said.

"We are going home."

Ailsa looked up at her, not knowing if she was serious or not.

"Really?" She whispered, "Home, my home?"

"Yes Ma, your home." Maria said, "We are all going home, together."

Ailsa looked around at the faces of her three children, as if she was seeing them for the first time. They all returned her look, each waiting for a reaction.

"Home," she repeated, and then slowly gradually a smile started to spread across her face, lighting it up with a new life. Her dull eyes awoke with a sparkle. She could feel her heart racing, pumping blood around her body, a sensation she had long forgotten.

"Really" she said, "now?" as her eyes took in the look of anticipation from her children and then they came to rest on the suitcases. Suddenly it all seemed very real.

"Are we really going this time Maria?"

"Yes, I told you we just had to wait till we had a little more money, and now, thanks to John and Cathy's help, we have."

For the first time they felt really important, as though they had truly achieved something. The delay in going home was now forgotten, only the present was important as they hugged their mother. And for once she didn't push them away.

Tears streamed down her face as she smiled. Cathy felt her mother's arms encase her, everyone was happy as excitement filled the air. It was as if the talk of going home had only ever been just talk, but now it was real and they couldn't quite grasp the enormous decision they had just made.

"Thank you," Ailsa said, "thank you. You will love it, I promise."

The following days Ailsa spoke incessantly about the large house, the countryside and all the other memories that came tumbling back,

The kids had never seen her so happy and it was so intoxicating that everyone suddenly seemed enriched with her feelings.

At last they were on the train; Maria had taken great care with their appearances. She had brought out all their new clothes. And now as they sat there, Maria felt very proud of them and of her own achievements. Cathy looked like an angel. Her hair had grown again and looked even more beautiful. The pale blue dress Maria had bought for her was a perfect match for her colouring, it brought out the warmth of her skin, and the golden tones of her hair.

As for John, Maria still couldn't contain his curls, but they were short and definitely adorable. He had on a smart summer shirt, one of the latest fashions from America. He felt really grown up and groovy, as he explained it, especially with his new sneakers and baseball cap. These had been a gift from one of the other traders, not just any trader but one who was totally infatuated with Maria, and would do anything for her. She just smiled and let him carry on adoring her.

The train didn't seem as big as she remembered it, or as plush. In fact, it looked quite tatty. Looking around she had to smile, as it struck her maybe the way they were dressed then, would make anything seem plush. Even her mother looked like a different woman. She was smartly dressed and had a kind of serenity about her that Maria had never seen before. But there was no mistaking the fact she did look ill; she was painfully thin, with deep dark circles around her eyes, and her skin had an unhealthy tinge of grey. Maria had stopped being angry with her, but she didn't feel sorry for her either. She really couldn't understand her mother and was hoping that when she met her grandparents things would fall into place. However, there was a little niggling thought at the back of her mind that things were not going to turn out as she was hoping.

It was a long journey. Cathy became tired, and John listless, though he did get excited when he saw animals in the fields as the train moved through the countryside. It was now May, the sun was shining the sky was blue and the earth was covered with flowers.

Maria had to admit she had missed the countryside. The sense of freedom she used to feel in the cool fresh morning air. Pictures of the tiny caravan that they had all lived in came to mind. She smiled ruefully, and it seemed such a lifetime away. Did she really break ice on the water to fill the pot so they could wash and make food and drink on the open fire?

"I bet I couldn't do it now," she said to herself.

"Do what Maria?"

"Just thinking John, remembering what it used to be like."

"I do that sometimes, especially now when I see the animals."

"I do it all the time," Cathy interrupted.

Both John and Maria turned to Cathy, each thinking the same. Cathy was not the type to think back, and she had been very young when they left.

"I remember the cold." she said.

They both smiled. That they could understand.

"Don't laugh, I remember everything. I remember Maria creeping out of the van dead early so she could make the fire before we got up so that we could be warm. And, she would make breakfast for us."

Maria smiled.

"I used to hear you whispering 'stupid wood' when it wouldn't light 'cause it was damp."

At this both Maria and John laughed, as they remembered it only too well. John added how she used to take them all down to the stream and they would splash and play.

By now Maria had tears in her eyes thinking of all the things that had happened in her life. It was nice to think there were some happy memories. Memories she had forgotten. And it was her little sullen Cathy of all people who had opened the door and let them all come flooding out.

The remainder of the journey was spent laughing as each one of them spoke of their own memories in turn. From hiding from their father, to annoying his girlfriends. Incredibly, what was sad then suddenly became a laugh now. It was Cathy who said she missed the three of them lying on a blanket under the caravan in the summer. They used to listen to the night sounds trying to figure out where it was coming from and who or what was making it and trying to count the stars.

"And Maria would tell us stories, do you remember John?"

"Yes Cathy," he replied quietly. He was now locked in his own memories. Like Maria, most of his memories had been hidden away. It seemed that only Cathy had missed her life and had never let go of it. John and Maria were now reliving it with her, amid lots of tears and laughter.

Chapter Eighteen.

They arrived. It was cold and blowing a strong wind which cut right through their clothes leaving them no protection against it. Maria had forgotten just how cold it was in Scotland, particularly in Inverness which was the capital of the highlands. They stood huddled together, each trying to pull their coats tighter around them, looking to see if anybody had arrived to pick them up.

Maria had written a very polite letter to her grandmother giving her precise details of their expected time of arrival, and adding that mother wasn't very well, and that if she knew how to get there herself she wouldn't be troubling her, but as it was Maria didn't know where her grandparents lived so it would be most appreciated if they would collect them all.

Finally after two hours, a young man appeared and led them out of the station, letting them each carry their own cases. He stopped beside a shiny Land Rover. John was totally in awe. He forgot how tired he was and ignored how ill-tempered the young man was, and went straight into raptures about the vehicle. Douglas responded to John's enthusiasm, introducing himself and helping them with their luggage.

During the journey back to the house he confided to Maria, that no-one was looking forward to their arriving. There had been nothing but angry scenes since they had received the letter.

Loud arguments followed by silence. The house and its staff had been plunged into a state of depression. Listening to him, Maria wondered if she had done the right thing. But then looking at her mother she knew she really didn't have a choice. And what about Cathy and John? This house was their inheritance. Why shouldn't they be there. She knew she would never be included in any kind of inheritance but it didn't bother her. She knew she was going to be rich anyway. No, they belonged here and she was going to live her own life. As much as she loved them, she knew she had to leave them. Her only hope was to make her grandparents want them, and she had the sneaky suspicion that all the arguments were probably about her.

It had now been three weeks since they had arrived and Maria was feeling the strain. It was everything her mother had said it was. The house was large, very grand and opulent. Food was plentiful and it was so clean it was frightening. Maria didn't know how to live anymore, there was nothing for her to do. Cathy became the re-incarnation of her mother and welcomed it. Her hair was styled the same as her mother's had been when she was her age and clothes that had belonged to her mother had been altered to fit. Cathy now looked like the perfect family clone, and even though Maria thought it was all rather sad, Cathy was perfectly happy. She loved the way her grandmother and her mother now spoke and copied every Scottish syllable. She even referred to Cannich as her home as though she had never been away from it.

When Maria had first arrived at Cannich she was quite amazed at how like her mother Cathy looked. There were photos everywhere of her mother's gentle smiling face. It was not the face of the mother she had known all her life and she could feel the bitterness creep in. She had tried so hard to make her mother love her and the others, had tried to make her happy, but not once could she ever remember her smiling. And now she walked about with one permanently on her face, along with Cathy who never left her side.

Maria was certain there was no new found love for her daughter it was probably that her mother had come to realise her mother had fallen in love with Cathy as soon as she had seen her. And Maria knew Ailsa would never ever do anything again to make her parents angry with her. In fact these last three weeks had worked out wonderfully for Ailsa! She had had time to spend with her mother and renew the love she so desperately needed because her father was away on business. He was also visiting his elder brother who was very poorly.

Smiling to herself, Maria had to admit it had been hard, very hard, but earning the money to bring them here had been for the best. At least for her mother and Cathy, they were so happy now in their own little world. Cathy had always been strange, in fact she used to annoy Maria sometimes because she was so like her mother, always complaining in a whining whimpering sort of way, yet doing nothing to improve her life. Maria often wanted to shake them both up to see if there was any real life in them. Yet even with all her faults, Maria missed her. They were in the same house but no longer met or communicated. She felt as though she had lost her sister and would never be needed again.

John, on the other hand, still professed love and gratitude every time he found something new! The house, the land, the loch, and how the deer would come down at dusk to drink. Finding discarded antlers on the hillside when he went for a walk with the gamekeeper. Every day was like a new adventure to him and he loved it. He wasn't privilege to the attention Cathy was receiving but he didn't care. He didn't need it. John was happy with the outdoor life. He was thirteen now and growing into a handsome young man. Again she had to admit she had done the right thing coming here. With good food his lean frame would soon fill out and she could see his natural tendency to the land. He loved it, along with all the animals and workers that had made it their home. His hair still looked too long, she smiled to herself. If it wasn't for the fine texture and colour, he had the same unruly curls she had.

Suddenly there were no giggles, no smiles, and no

happiness. She was different there was no use in her pretending otherwise, she was like a fish out of water. No one spoke to her, her grandmother lavished love and attention on her mother and Cathy and even John. But when it came to her she was ignored, excluded and made to feel unwelcome. This was something Maria couldn't quite understand, she was fifteen going on sixteen, she was a young woman who had worked hard for the past few years to keep her small family together. Even before that she couldn't remember a time when she hadn't looked after John and Cathy and now, when she had succeeded in what she had set out to do, she felt ignored and shunned.

Maria had united her family, but she was alone, she had lost everything. She had lost her family. As the true meaning of everything became apparent, the realisation of not belonging overwhelmed her.

Her life had always had a reason, a goal. Even her hate and anger had had an outlet. Now though being here, whose fault had it really been? Could she continue blaming her father? Oh, he was in the wrong, but did that exclude her grandparents for not doing what was the right thing to do? After all, it was their daughter, whom they professed to love, who was given to a total stranger with no means of gainful employment to keep her. They had to accept some responsibility for the family's miserable existence of a life.

As the tension mounted within her, Maria could feel all the frustrations and hurt of how she was being treated and how unfair it all was. What gave them the right to ignore her? Ailsa was supposed to be her mother, and as for her grandmother, she had no right what so-ever in treating her so badly. Nobody had the right to ignore her and refuse to accept her very existence, nobody. Her temper began to rise, she didn't know what to do, but it was too strong to go away. Soft laughter filtered through the door. Incensed she followed the sound to the library where she saw her mother and grandmother both looking at yet another photo of the young Ailsa. Maria couldn't help herself, storming over she shouted at them both to grow up.

"How dare you talk to me like that" her grandmother retorted angrily. "Who do you think you are?"

"Well, that's the million dollar question isn't it? Who am I, your daughter?" she said, pointing to Ailsa. "Or your granddaughter perhaps? Oh no, sorry, you don't recognise me. Come to think of it, you don't either, do you mother dear?" Maria could hear her voice rising but she no-longer cared.

"Stop it, stop it this moment, if your grandfather was here he wouldn't let you speak to me like this."

"But he isn't here is he? He's never been here for us, has he mother? Your own children have never met him, have we? He's no better than that fellow you married, remember our dear father who also abandoned us."

Maria felt the full force of a hand across her face. Her temper was suddenly replaced by a cold hatred; it shone wildly in her dark eyes. Her grandmother recoiled in terror as she felt it; it was almost tangible in the air. Maria quietly and purposely faced her square on, and raising her hand smacked her grandmother with such a force, she fell to the floor. Distant memories had come flooding back as Maria once more touched her face and felt the throb of pain.

Ailsa was crying as she helped her mother up, at first too shocked to speak. But, as she regained her composure and opened her mouth to speak, Maria interrupted her.

"Don't ever raise your hand to me again." she said in the kind of voice no-one should ever hear.

Ailsa could feel her daughter's animosity and started to cry. She didn't understand why Maria was so angry, and the ferocity of her words stunned her. She had never seen her daughter behave like this, and was frightened in case mother told her father. He was due home tomorrow and if he knew about this he would be angry and make her leave again. She couldn't stand that thought and threw herself into the arms of her mother, crying.

"I'm sorry mother, I'm sorry, I told you she was strange. Please don't blame me will you. Don't tell father. It wasn't my fault."

As she felt her mother's arms around her, stroking her hair like she did when she was young, Ailsa knew her mother still loved her and would keep her safe. But turning to Maria, Ailsa was still confused as to why she had struck her mother. Why she had nearly had them all thrown out again. She couldn't bear the thought and clung to her mother as though it was a matter of life or death.

"See what you've done." her grandmother said, "You are not fit to be part of this family."

But it was the finality in her mother's voice as she said "Why are you here? You don't belong, you never have."

That's what hurt Maria the most, like the last wound you receive before you die. This was the pain Maria now felt.

Maria walked blindly into the hills, tears streaming down her face. Her head ached as the words repeated themselves over and over again. "You don't belong"

The mountains still had snow-capped peaks and the rugged hills spread out before her, but in the midst of this wonderful countryside was a great big concrete wall, the dam. She stood there looking, yet seeing nothing.

"Why?" she asked herself. "Why?"

The words seemed to haunt her wherever she went. The water swished against the solid wall of concrete as it climbed higher and higher, until it almost reached the top where Maria now stood. Its presence seemed to break through into her mind, reminding her of something ugly, something that shouldn't be there. Yet she also knew it was needed and that without it the whole of the glen would be flooded. Its rolling river would then be free to destroy everything.

She crossed from one side of the bridge to the other and her eyes became aware of the mountains in the distance. The snow she thought was like looking at the icing on the tip of a cake that had run down into thin narrow veins, spreading itself through the green and purple heather, and into the large expanse of Scottish Pine that covered the ground. It was wild and rugged. You could feel its relationship with nature. They were together in a kind of amnesty. As her eyes drifted on down, the Glen opened up. A large loch appeared, it seemed almost unreal as it sat peacefully just below the sloping hills. Maria started to walk down towards it. It had a welcoming aura of comfort as dusk started slowly to envelop her.

From the shadows a great stag appeared, followed by a slowly moving deer, making their way down to drink from the cool waters of the loch. Each majestic in its own right, male and female...

"It's beautiful, isn't it?"

Maria turned, not expecting to see anybody, she was momentarily speechless.

"Did you know, when you leave this beautiful loch you have a nine mile walk down the side of the mountain?" said a male voice.

"I can take care of myself".

"And it will soon be dark," he said, ignoring her. "It's a thin, dangerous, winding, twisting road so it is, and very steep in parts. Definitely not for the likes of a young city girl like yourself," he added

"Who said I'm from the city and anyway why should you care?"

"That's no way to talk to a distant relative."

"Being a relative puts you lower down my list."

"Who's upset you then? I thought I heard stories of a happy reunion between mother and daughter."

"Look, I don't know who you are or what you want, just go away. And by the way, you heard right only you got the wrong daughter."

"I'm James" he said sombrely. "Are you always this friendly?"

"Yes. Are you supposed to mean something to me?" She

asked starting to get annoyed at his intrusion.

"Yeah, cousins, three times removed I think. You're Grandfather and mine are brothers."

"Well, I don't know your grandfather and I've disowned mine. What does that tell you?"

"What's your name?"

"Maria."

"Well Maria, I think we have just become closer."

She studied him closely as his eyes took on a mischievous look and his lips spread into a generous smile.

"I don't like any of them either," he said. "Only it's them that have disowned me".

Maria was intrigued, "Why?"

"That conversation is for another day."

"How do you know there will be another day?

"There has to be, we don't have anyone else to talk to,"

She couldn't help it; she just had to return his smile. It was starting to get dark and Maria realised he was right. Steep drops appeared at the side of the road when you least expected them. James didn't seem to notice, he was too busy pointing out various cottages and crofts that dotted the mountainside in the failing light. He obviously loved and knew the area but Maria had come up here in a temper. She wanted to wind down, to get away from them all. She had walked for hours and now realised she would never find her way back. Already the winding roads were blending in with their surroundings and, apart from the sporadic light of the moon, it was becoming increasingly dark.

"James," she said "stop talking."

He smiled "Sorry, I get carried away. It's not that often I have the chance to show off my favourite part of the world, especially to one so pretty." Maria scowled. "You don't like compliments do you?" "No!" she said.

"Okay, don't look so worried, I won't do it again."

"That's not why I'm worried." she said impatiently. "In case you haven't noticed, it's getting dark?"

"I already said that."

"Yes, I know. Now tell me, what we are going to do?"

"We? I'm going home. I pointed it out to you before remember, the little white cottage nestling in the hills above the Loch." He was tormenting her and thoroughly enjoying it. "How beautiful she is," he thought. "How absolutely wild and angry, she looked. Her face is like a mirror of many images, all falling together, all conflicting, she really was quite extraordinary" he concluded, totally captivated and intrigued by her.

I'm sorry," Maria said trying to control herself. She guessed he was playing with her but couldn't retaliate. She was in the middle of nowhere and knew she definitely wouldn't like to be alone out there. And anyway, she was starting to feel tired and very cold.

"What do you suggest I do cousin dear?" she said sarcastically.

"I suggest you come back with me."

She stopped and glared at him hard. Gone was the friendly banter as she felt the old hostility rise up inside her.

"Hey, don't look like that. I have a spare room. You'll be safe, honest, cross my heart."

She could see his face in the moonlight. She had over-reacted, she realised that. He was family, after all, and in some strange way, she trusted him.

The next morning found them happily eating breakfast together out on the patio, completely at ease and relaxed in each other's company. It had been a good night, a night Maria would remember for the rest of her life.

They had talked, laughed and sang. James filled her in on the family's secrets except when it came to himself. "That's for another night" he had said laughing, "Too much too soon will send you running to the hills." But he did tell her he wanted to be a musician and go to America, become rich and famous and party with all the stars.

"From what I've seen I think that's probably enough to label you a black sheep of the family, right next to me." Maria said.

And they had both laughed so hard, tears had rolled down their faces.

"Oh Maria, I haven't felt this happy for as long as I can remember. I can honestly say I have never had anyone to talk to, really talk to, that is."

"No, me neither"

"And what are your plans?" he asked her gently.

"Me? I'm just going to be rich, the fame you can have"

"Deal." he said.

Chapter Nineteen.

Returning to the big house Maria was once again struck by the sheer power of it. Each room had its own character. Dining rooms, breakfast rooms, lounge, a library and three kitchens. "Who would want three kitchens?" she thought. The list was endless; bedrooms, each with their own washing facilities lined the upstairs landing. Above those, in the attics as Maria called them, were seven more rooms for the workers. However, when the hall had been first built they were called servants' quarters.

Maria had to admit that it was truly a magnificent building. She couldn't bring herself to call it a home. It was too big, a lodge, a great hall, a hotel even, but definitely not a home. One of the bay windows stood twenty feet tall and fifteen feet wide with doors that opened out onto the most beautiful patio flanked by a very natural looking cultured garden that seemed to slope down into vast fields with no end. As you sat there watching the sun go down, it was quite remarkable. The best thing, she smiled, was the fact that it was large enough to enjoy without having to meet anyone. Everyone could find their own space.

After the fight with her grandmother and the consequent follow-up with her grandfather, Maria had decided to go back to Manchester, but now she pondered. She had heard Tim was doing alright. Trade was slow in the summer months as they had forecast, but they were still making all their targets. So she felt there was no need to rush back because then she would have the added expense of a room to live in, and why waste money?

Besides, the deeper part of her which liked to retaliate and do things right, couldn't agree to her grandparents telling her to go. They had never done anything for her, so why should she listen to them. This was as much her home as it was Cathy's and John's. But the real reason she wanted to stay was James.

Maria avoided her mother and grandparents. There was always an altercation and they made it clear that they didn't want her.

"Tough," she had said to her grandfather that morning.

He had turned red in the face and spluttered his words in temper as he failed to intimidate her. To Maria it meant nothing, he could shout all he liked, for one thing she had learned from Michael was the power of being a minor.

"You can't throw me out," she had said coldly and deliberately to him. "I am a minor, it's against the law. So I might decide to stay until I'm sixteen."

His eyes had bulged and his colour deepened.

"He wasn't a very handsome man," Maria chuckled to herself, and boy was he annoyed at being manipulated by the one person he blamed for all his unhappiness in life.

But she was right. He couldn't put her out. It would be sociably unacceptable.

"Then I don't want to see your face until the day you leave, you don't belong"

Not very long ago those words would have hurt so much, but now, all that had changed. Meeting James had been a life changing experience for Maria. He was in the same situation, he didn't live with anyone and wasn't wanted by the family, though she didn't know why. She had tried to find out but no-one would talk about him. Maria thought it was very strange. He was so nice, so gentle and unaffected. She thought he looked about twenty five, ten years older than her, but he had the kind of nature that made him appear younger.

Maria would go up to his cottage at night and stay and talk. Sometimes, he would play the guitar and Maria would hum along with him. It was wonderful. She loved his way of life. She felt part of it, though not once did he make any improper advances towards her. At first Maria thought it was because they were related, but then she realised that they were so far removed there wasn't really much family blood between them. But she felt safe and happy being with him and that's all that mattered. As time went on though Maria did have fleeting thoughts as to why he never made any advances. He obviously liked her, he told her so. In fact, she received more compliments from James in a few weeks than she'd had in her whole life. They would drink wine under the stars, or lie in front of the open fire on a large furry rug, relaxed, even snuggling into each other before falling asleep. But always he respected her person.

Soon, Maria's mind started playing tricks on her. She believed she was falling in love, feeling him holding her, protecting her and never letting anything or anyone ever hurt her again. She would fantasise about staying in the cottage forever and shutting out the whole world. Although James held her tenderly and lovingly, it was always as a brother might, not a lover. In her mind, Maria had started to imagine him as her lover. He was beautiful, in a feminine sort of way, unlike David, who still invaded her dreams but who she was beginning to accept that because he had never written was probably happily married by now. "He might even have children," she thought wistfully.

Maria picked up the wine glass and drank it in one.

"What's to do?"

"Nothing," she answered quietly.

"Please tell me. You can say anything to me. You know that, it hurts me to see you looking so sad?

She looked at James, there really wasn't one ounce of him that wasn't good. His eyes, his smile, his whole face seemed genuinely concerned. As truthful as she had been about feelings for David and her unfortunate relationship with Michael, Maria couldn't tell James how much she needed to be held, and loved, if only for one night. But that is exactly what happened, as though they shared the same soul. They each felt the other's need and James, in all tenderness, loved her slowly, quietly and emotionally. When she lay in his arms tired and relaxed, her body had a light floating feeling. A feeling of love, not sex or passion but of togetherness she never knew could exist, and with a smile on her face she fell into a deep sleep.

Chapter Twenty.

Her body felt ravaged by pain, by a feeling she couldn't or wouldn't accept and a sadness so great she felt as though she was going to die, so great it was. Desperately she tried to pack her bag, she had to get away. All the time her tears fell uncontrollably down her face, her eyes were glazed and her mind a blank but still she continued to pack her clothes neatly away in the suitcase. As she lifted the case onto the floor her eyes drifted through the window beyond the heavy gold curtains. In the distance she could see her snow peaked mountains as fresh tears cascaded down. She was heartbroken.

"Why God, why isn't there anyone I can love, what do I have to do? I just need one small sign, anything, help me to understand." she demanded.

Then she threw herself onto the bed as the tears came fast and furious. She was no longer in control, she had had enough. The pain she felt was so intense she thought it would never end. As she lay on the bed, her tears subsiding, her thoughts tried desperately to unravel the knotted threads in her mind, the confusion, and the inability to comprehend or understand why or how anyone could be like that.

Maria stared at the ceiling, it was a beautiful ceiling, why that should invade her thoughts she didn't know. Because at this time of her life she really didn't care.

Desperately she tried to piece everything together, but it was hard, she remembered how he had turned towards her, tears in his eyes, his voice barely a whisper.

"I am so sorry Maria, so sorry."

"Please don't say that," she had pleaded.

"You don't understand."

"What's there to understand, we did what we did, it's the most natural thing in the world for two people who love each other to do it. You do love me James don't you?"

"I truly love you Maria, I just can't find the right words to explain myself. Maria, I have never made love to a woman before."

"That's all right," she breathed with relief. "I wondered what you were going to say."

She reached up to kiss him.

"Maria listen, no, I'm homosexual."

She pulled away in shock, it was something she had heard about, but didn't understand. They were people who were strange, abnormal, it was unhealthy, and also against the law of man and God. She had heard all the stories, but had never met one.

"No you are wrong, you can't be, you're not one of them" she had cried. "You are good and kind and loving, and you are so normal, how can you be a homosexual?"

A fresh flood of tears ran down her cheeks as she remembered the pain she saw in his face and realised it had been all her fault. He had tried so many times to tell her, she knew that now, but her need of wanting him, to feel the closeness of them together had closed her mind to his feelings. Suddenly she knew. The situation had arisen because of her and she was devastated, just thinking about it overwhelmed her. She had been so selfish.

"I'm sorry James I'm sorry. You were there for me, comforted me the way I needed comforting, I thought only of myself and still you loved me." Maria realised James was probably the only person who had ever really loved her, and how had she repaid him? She had never, in all her life, felt so bad about herself, as she did then.

"What have I done?" she cried, as the tears continued to flow.

Taking her pale blue cardigan she threw it around her shoulder, pulled on her shoes and ran to the door. Maria now knew his was probably the sweetest, purist love any one had ever given her and she had thrown it back in his face. He had been devastated.

She had to go to him, to find him, to tell him she was sorry. On and on she ran, wanting the wind to lift her up and take her to him. Suddenly, there in answer to her prayers, she saw him sat beside the loch. Head down, hands over his face his knees brought up under his chin he sat motionless watching the water. She could feel his sadness as she approached and felt wretched. James was one of life's gentle people who gave only happiness and love and she felt as though she had destroyed that. She remembered his face as she ran crying saying awful things to him that morning, leaving him alone broken and dejected.

"I'm sorry James, I'm sorry," she cried running up to him.

He stood and holding his arms wide he looked as though he was seeing a vision, unable to fully accept she had come back to him. But as his arms encircled her and she cried into his chest, his own tears mingled with hers. And there they stood as if time had frozen, giving them the chance to embrace life once again as two people who just loved each other in their own special way.

Maria's birthday was coming up, but there was to be no celebrations, as her grandparents still wouldn't acknowledge her. Her mother lived another life and Cathy, in the few moments when she did take notice of Maria, was either nice or nasty. She thanked her for bringing her home and then the next day she could change and blame her for making them all live in poverty. John was John, he never changed. He seemed to love everyone, but he especially loved the land and in a moment of sadness threw his arms around Maria and begged her to forgive him for wanting to stay there and leave her to go back to Manchester alone. Maria was touched that at least one member of her family loved her.

The following evening as she lay quietly in James's arms in front of the open fire, feeling relaxed and happy. He turned to her, and looking quite serious said. "We are going to have a celebration before you return to Manchester." He smiled, "But," he said, "We are also going to give them the biggest shock in the world."

Maria laughed, but said "No thanks, the only celebration I want is to be here with you. When I leave this place I want my last memories to be happy."

"Then do one thing for me Maria?"

"What?"

"Don't be annoyed, and don't say anything without thinking for at least five minutes, promise."

"Okay, I promise."

He took his watch out and placed it on the table, she laughed out loud.

"This looks serious," she said.

"Will you marry me?"

"What?"

"Five minutes you promised."

"Yes, but."

"Think about it Maria. I love you dearly and you will make me a very happy man, even if it's in name only. I do love you dearly. Besides, what if you have a baby, we did all the right things." he laughed.

Maria went to speak, but he pointed to the watch.

"Do this Maria, and if at any time you want a divorce you know you can have one. I will never marry, and what I have is yours, I don't have anything yet not until I'm rich and famous. Think hard about it, Maria. Once you go back to Manchester you might need the security of a marriage licence. It's almost 1957 and yes times are changing. But women who live on their own especially young ones, are still looked down on."

"I don't know what to say."

"Say yes, we are doing it for all the right reasons and you know I love you."

"I love you too James; you're the nicest, most decent person I have ever known."

"Is that a yes, then?"

"What about my age?"

He could see by her face she was coming around to the idea, and he knew it would be for the best as she would have more security when she went back. People wouldn't always be asking her how old she was and that alone would make life easier.

"In Scotland, you can marry at sixteen." He smiled.

"But what about us being related?"

"No I checked it out, just in case you said yes."

"I don't know what to say."

"You have said that already, say yes now. Seriously though Maria we could be having a baby."

"I don't think I will be having a baby, but if we did get married it would have to be our secret."

"Why?"

"Because when I leave, I will be happy and they are not

going to spoil it. You are already the black sheep of the family, I won't give them any cause to ridicule our decision."

"Is that a yes then?" he almost shouted whirling her around. "You won't be sorry."

"I know. When you're rich and famous…"

"Absolutely, just wait till I finish my studies, I did tell you I was studying music didn't I?"

"Yes you did, now tell me what we have to do?"

Like a couple of children giggling they made their plans. James couldn't go to the big house, as he called it. His own parents had died in an accident and his grandfather lived out in Fort William. So he was free to plan anything he wanted.

Maria on the other hand, had to take her birth certificate out of her mother's box discreetly, and go with him to put the wedding banns in. They were to marry on her sixteenth birthday which was just three weeks away. They picked a quiet little church in Nairn, which was on the coast and very popular for holiday makers and visitors. No one would know them or ask questions.

It was a beautiful day in February, cool crisp and very bright with the sun shining proudly. Together they stood alongside two of James's friends who had been sworn to secrecy, looking every bit like a young couple who loved each other. Afterwards they hired a car and drove back to the cottage on the mountain. There, along with his friends, Maria spent a wonderful night. A large open fire and a clear blue sky with lots of stars, soft music played by James and his friends all added to the magic of the moment.

As they hummed together, James looked at Maria and started to sing a song he had written especially for her. With tears in his eyes and words which came straight from his heart he sang quietly, emotionally, lovingly.

My Love is my gift, I give to you It's pure in heart, and will always be true Moments of Love, Will always be there Through time and space, Thoughts we'll share For my Love is my Gift, I give to you Forever and ever, it will always be true.

The memory of that night would stay with Maria forever. Taking off her shoes she would slowly walk and enjoy the freedom she always felt when she did. It had to be one of her greatest pleasures. Sometimes she would hum to the birds or the insects, other times she would be deep in thought. But one thing she did know and that was, that she truly loved this part of the world. After only six months she felt as though she belonged. She had found something in her life that had been missing. A kind of happiness which she never knew existed. An understanding of herself, and an understanding of real love.

Coming to the edge of the Loch, Maria sat contented. Her fingers became entwined as she felt the grass. It was not the soft silky grass which was found in the city, but more of a strong, hard and enduring grass. She smiled to herself

"I would prefer to think I am like you." she said admiringly. "An inner strength as James said is better than anything." She laughed to herself. "What have you done to me James?" she said softly thoughtfully, "I am becoming a deep thinker, just like you."

As Maria lay back her head resting on the cool grass, her thoughts took her back over the past few months.

Her temper, the arguments with her mother and grandmother, she shouldn't have hit her, she realised that, but then she had driven her to the edge. On reflection, Maria thanked her for doing that because if she hadn't, she wouldn't have run away and therefore would never have met James.

James was wonderful. He was everything she had ever admired in a person, as well as being talented clever and philosophical.

"The words you used were so, how would you say, I don't know," she admitted "I want to learn like you James. As you put it, I have met the brick wall and I've turned and faced life." Maria became quiet as her mind went over his words. He was like no-one she had ever met.

"What was it you said? Accept people for what they are, not for what you want them to be. You don't have to love them. It's your life, it's up to you how you live it."

With a contented sigh Maria made her way back to the house. But then she saw her grandfather in the garden. She stood watching him and all her good intentions were fighting hard against an almost uncontrollable urge to hurl abuse at him. Instead, taking a deep controlled breath, she quietly approached him. He turned, his face dropped, obviously expecting someone else, disappointment was written all over him. Then just as quickly it turned to anger, and irritation.

It was all Maria could do to stop her temper from flaring up again, she studied him silently.

"What do you want? From what I have heard there is nothing about you that includes anything decent. You have no respect for anyone or anything." he said in disgust as he stared at her

"You have to earn respect," she said pleasantly, "and there's no one here that I know of, who deserves it."

Maria spoke quietly, trying to understand what James had said. Her grandfather was what he was, she didn't have to like him, but she had to get rid of all the pent up emotions she had. And she stared at this old man with his withered face having spent too long in the bleak Scottish weather. Eyes that held no emotion and lips that didn't know how to smile. She felt sorry for him. His whole demeanour was one of anger and defeat and also, she thought, one of complete sadness. It was as if life had given him nothing and he had given life nothing, that there was only emptiness. Maria also realised nothing was going to change him now. The resemblance between him and her mother was striking. Apart from the physical likeness there was the same tendencies of feelings and mental attitude.

"What are you smiling at girl?"

Maria hadn't realised she was smiling.

"You remind me of my mother," she said simply.

"Well you don't," he said vindictively. "You look like that man who spawned you. Why are you still here, you don't belong. We don't want you." His voice sounded cold and hard, "You destroyed this family."

Maria studied him.

"No more brick walls." she said.

"What?"

"What are you going on about girl, are you wrong in the head?"

Where once she would have retaliated she now smiled.

"I belong where ever I am, because I am me, but don't worry I won't be staying long."

"Good, your grandmother will be glad to hear it."

"Careful, you will be accepting the fact I am related to you!"

"What do you want, why are you disturbing me, I don't want to talk to you."

"That's okay grandfather dear, I will leave as soon as I can, but you see I am too young. How will I find somewhere to live. I have no money for rent and no means to get some. If I am lucky I might earn a living but then again I might not. Would you let me starve in the gutter? Don't answer that, I remember you sent my mother away penniless."

"I did not," he shouted. "Your mother had a very healthy dowry when she got married."

"Okay, give me a dowry."

"Why should I?"

"Because then I would go and you need never see me again."

"I could just throw you out."

"True, but in England I would still be a minor, and you wouldn't want me to stay around here now would you?"

They both stood silently staring into each other's eyes.

"How much do you want?" he eventually said in a defeated attitude.

"Whatever a good dowry is, you have to be seen to be fair and I promise I'll tell everyone I'm married."

"You probably could, I'm sure lying comes easily."

"Believe me dear grandfather, when I tell people I'm married I will believe it myself." She smiled as she thought of James and that lovely little ceremony they had had.

Studying her, he realised there was something about her he didn't really understand, but he desperately wanted his wife to be happy again and if that meant buying her off, then so be it.

"Okay." he said. "Come to the study tomorrow." Then he turned his back and walked away.

Maria felt like laughing out loud. James was right, she did feel better, she felt free, nothing, could hurt her now.

Chapter Twenty One.

The train made its way cutting through the country side. Maria felt inwardly at peace. When she had said farewell to James in the cottage, she had decided, it was the most perfect place in the whole world. It was somewhere, where she had found real love. For some unknown reason she sensed she would never see him again, but to her he would always be there, in the cottage.

When she took the cheque from her grandfather, Maria had felt no guilt whatsoever. She had gone into Inverness and deposited it in the bank on High Street. She liked Inverness, it was small and friendly and she thought that the way the River Ness ran through it, bringing its clear blue water into your life, was just wonderful. When she was in Salford, sitting beside the River Irwell had always been her place to go when she needed peace, but the River Ness had been peace itself.

As the train picked up speed, she realised she was sorry to be going as part of her would always belong there.

"But it's time to move on," she sighed.

Maria had wanted to be on her own when the time had come to leave, and now she was glad she had made that decision. Saying goodbye was something she couldn't do. Because underneath Maria knew her life would never be the same again. Her mother and brother and sister belonged in Inverness and they knew nothing about James. It was as she wanted it. But some part of her still hurt.

Still, as she travelled further towards Manchester, her mind became active, thinking about Tim and Laura and how the business was doing. Life would seem strange without Cathy and John, she knew that. Even her mother would leave a void in her life.

"It had to happen," she told herself. "Life changes, I'm different now, no more emotional hang-ups it's time I lived my life."

Leaving the train at Manchester, Maria started to walk. She needed to do this, to remember how far she had come in such a short time. She had taken her family home, got married, and was coming back to her own business. "And," she said to herself with pride. "I now have a very healthy bank balance and I'm still only sixteen,"

Little Emma threw her arms around Maria as did Paul, and Laura was positively happy to see her, Ada also had tears in her eyes as she welcomed her home.

"Home?" Maria enquired.

"You didn't think I would let your room go, did you?" Ada said smiling. "Come on, I'll show you."

Inside, Ada proudly showed Maria the newly refurbished room, it looked nothing like it had been and for this Maria was so grateful.

"It wasn't all my doing," she said, "It was Laura and Tim. They just kept finding nice pieces to bring in from the market."

Maria was speechless. The bed had a lovely pink and grey blanket draped across it. In front of the fire, was a rich red rug, and on the table there was the most delicate lace tablecloth she had ever seen. It had little red roses embroidered all around the edges.

"It's beautiful," she said.

"Welcome home," came a voice from the door. It was Tim.

"I really do feel as though I have come home." She said "I'm speechless, thank you, all of you, thank you," and then the tears came, tears of happiness that knew no boundaries.

That evening, Maria spoke of everything that had happened. Of James and how she loved him, not in the girlfriend - boyfriend way but in a very special way.

"He helped me to grow up," she laughed.

"How did he manage that? You say you met hostility from every one you met, yet he convinced you to be nice to them all. That I find hard to believe. That's not the Maria we know and love!"

"Well it was not exactly like that, Tim," Maria said laughing "because, let's face it, I couldn't be nice if I tried with the family. But I did learn how to dismiss them from my mind. I have more control now and I think it's because he helped me to understand.

"Come on then, tell us how?" Tim said intrigued.

"He said I should accept that there are times when life is bad. And that sometimes the people you love will hurt you. There is nothing good about unfair behaviour from someone you love. Or from someone who persistently hurts you. But then he said, 'Isn't it all in the mind? You believe what you want to believe. And to be fair, most people know what they want to believe. To blame others is just another way of giving up. If you leave the realities of life and run then you come up against a brick wall. And it is then you are forced to face the truth, to face life, and then what do you do?' I said I didn't really know."

"And then what did he say?" Laura asked

"He said I had come up against my brick wall. He said it was time I turned and faced whatever it was that was out there, but it had to be my life. To live a life where I didn't expect people to be what I wanted them to be, but to accept them for what they are. I don't have to love them. I don't have to have anything to do with them. In fact I can just clear my mind of them. He said that then I will be in control, then I will be living my own life and no one will ever be able to hurt me again.

"Wow, he seems like a very deep thinking kind of person." Tim said.

"No, he isn't anything like that," she smiled wistfully.

"You haven't fallen for him have you, Maria, and are not saying?" Laura asked softly.

"I probably love him in a way I will never love another. He's a kind and sensitive person who loves life. He's also a musician."

"But"...................

"Why do you say that?"

"Because I can tell from the way you are talking there is a 'but'."

"You are right Tom, he has learnt the hard way. He ran into his brick wall when he was only sixteen like me. He's twenty five now."

"What happened to him?" Ada asked

"He lost both parents when he was two years old. His grandfather brought him up. His grandfather is my grandfather's brother. Apparently the farm and all the land was once owned by his grandfather but after James said he didn't want to work on the land he gave it all to my grandfather."

"There must be more to it than that Maria. No-one gives away everything they own just because they don't have an heir to work it?" Tim said.

"It was a terrible blow to learn he preferred music to the land and oh did I tell you he was also homosexual."

"A queer" they all repeated together in shock.

"Yes! And apparently, in Scotland it's just like here only worse. It's not even spoken about, let alone accepting one into your own family. It's classed as a sin against God and man. He was disowned and disinherited. That's how my grandparents got everything.

"Gosh, how sad," Laura whispered.

"Yes, he said it was awful, he was shunned by his family and friends. No one in the whole of the country side would look at him let alone speak to him. He was totally alone until he found a friend in Nairn, that's a place just outside Inverness. The friend introduced him to some musicians, a new philosophy of life and the brick wall. He said he has never looked back since, and no longer carries emotional baggage around; he is free to live."

Everyone remained silent as they thought of what they had just heard. It made life seem so simple.

"I suppose each and every one of us has emotional baggage to carry around." Ada said quietly as if she was talking to herself.

"Where is he now Maria?"

"He lives in a beautiful cottage high up in a glen, Tim, where there are snow peaked mountains and the most wonderful loch that has deer and stags drinking from it."

"He doesn't sound that poor to me, Maria."

"It was owned by his parents Ada; they left him that and a small legacy, which has paid him to go through 'The School of Music'. He said I can use the cottage any time I want to. He's going away to America, to seek his fame and fortune," she added.

Maria omitted to mention her night of passion, or the fact she had married him. She needed more time herself to know, accept and understand what she had actually done. But one thing she did know, and that was that she wasn't sorry. Whatever had happened between them had been done with love. And apart from anything else, he had given her an understanding of how to live her life and for that she would always be grateful.

The evening finished with Maria feeling satisfied and happy. Tim, Laura, Paul and little Emma, together with Ada, all seemed to be an integrated part of her life now. She loved them all; she was with people who loved her for what she was. Together they would go forward, they would be rich. From then on, nothing and no one could ever hurt her again. With this thought, she closed her eyes, pulled the luxurious soft blanket around her neck and snuggled down to sleep, a smile on her face.

The following day brought sunshine and a very happy and relaxed Maria. She had a kind of lightness inside her that she couldn't explain. She stood by the stall. They had worked hard dressing it but the end result was fantastic. She couldn't help but be impressed. It looked amazing, the colours of the knitwear all came together in a soft and striking appearance, enhanced by the artful display of pairing the garments up which gave a very professional finish. Together they stood, each feeling very proud of themselves.

"That was the easy bit, now we have to sell it all." Maria laughed.

"No problem" Tim answered.

Very soon, the customers came. Many of them were mothers pushing prams having just been to school to drop off the older children. They now browsed around the market. Some bought, some didn't but Maria realised they looked enviously at the many styles and Maria knew they were picturing themselves wearing them. They would stop to finger the soft wool, enjoy happy banter but admit they didn't quite have enough money.

"I try to put it away, love, you know, but after a couple of weeks there is always something that seems more important and then it's gone again. But I'm determined to have one of them there Mohair cardigans, so I am," said one wistful mother, who looking longingly at the soft pink one.

"Tim how often do we hear that story?"

"Oh, I would say at least twenty times a day, why?"

"Well I was just thinking if they can afford to put so much away why can't they have the goods first?"

"What are you saying Maria?"

"I'm saying we take a chance and start giving credit."

"I don't know about that, what if we don't see them

again?"

"No we will do it properly, we will have a collector who will call for it every week. Build it in the price, keeping it as low as we can but with lots of incentives."

"Sounds good," Tim said thoughtfully.

"We can do it ourselves. To begin with, Tim, say twenty per cent interest. They pay ten per cent weekly and when the account starts to come down they can purchase more goods without increasing their outlay." Maria was positively buzzing with excitement the more she thought about it.

"We will then have a permanent on-going income," Tim said beginning to understand the implications of how much their income could grow.

"But what if they don't pay?"

"Tim, for every customer they introduce, we will work out a bonus. Believe me, if they don't have the money they will soon find a friend, and then they won't have to worry about that week's repayment."

"Sounds too good to be true, but you are right Maria it does have all the makings of us bringing in some serious money.

"Yes and as it grows, we'll employ someone on commission only. Firstly, on what they sell and secondly on what they collect in.

They can have a van with a full complement of knitwear; the customers will be able to buy there and then. Think of it Tim, selling every day of the week, earning money every day.

"What is your aim?" Tim said smiling.

"We are going to be very rich; we will expand, buy a large store, and ask the customers what they want." She laughed "and we will sell it, then the collector collects the money.

"Maria you are fantastic, it would definitely work except for one minor detail."

"What's that?" she said feeling a little deflated.

"We need capital to fund all the merchandise, until we recoup some back from the weekly payments."

"Don't worry about that Tim," she said relieved, "I have it all in hand."

Tim never ceased to be amazed at Maria, she knew what she wanted and somehow managed to get the means of accomplishing it.

"Maria" he said, "I am with you one hundred per cent."

"That's better" she said, "because I know it is going to be good. In fact, it's going to be spectacular. You know what Tim?"

"What?"

"We are going to be rich," she laughed, "very rich."

Chapter Twenty Two.

"Maria talk to me, are you pregnant?"

Maria sighed, "Yes Laura, I think I am."

"You want to talk about it?"

"No, but believe me Laura, I love the father and he loves me. This baby is definitely a gift from God. And I am going to do all I can to be a good mother."

"And the father, does he know?"

"No, but he will. For now though I would prefer not to say who he is. Sometime in the future I will tell you Laura, but I am not ready yet, I have to sort it all out in my head. You do understand, don't you?"

"Yes of course I do, and no matter what you decide I will always be here."

Maria hugged her "Thank you," she said. "Thank you."

"Meanwhile, you will have to look after yourself. This latest project as you call it is doing very well. You'll be able to employ somebody soon."

"You mean 'we' can employ some one. It's yours and

Tim's business as much as mine you know."

Laura put her arms around her and held her close. Maria felt terribly emotional, she wasn't used to being touched or held and was quite overwhelmed. Tears threatened her eyes as she realised just how comforting it felt.

"You will have to take it easier Maria, and don't worry about anything. We will all love and help look after this baby."

Maria felt so grateful at having so much support around her. When she had first realised that she could be pregnant, her mind played games. Could she ever expect to make a good mother? How would she know what to do? Now though, after talking to everyone, she felt more confident. Now she realised they were like one big happy family, and patting her tummy breathed deeply and happily. This baby she knew was going to be surrounded by people who loved him. Maria already felt as though she was having a little boy.

It was a boy. A normal delivery with no undue complications and Maria, together with Tim, Laura, Ada and little Emma and Paul all looked at him in amazement, he seemed so small.

"He's beautiful," Maria whispered, she felt like crying with happiness, he was her son, she could hardly believe it. Never had she ever felt anything, like she felt at that moment when they placed her son in her arms. Nothing had prepared her for the joy and love that overwhelmed her.

"He's gorgeous," Ada whispered.

Then Maria laughed, "he's going to have the same unruly black hair that I have."

Then his little fingers clenched into a tiny fist as he declared with a loud cry he was hungry.

"Just like you," Paul said innocently, and they all laughed.

Over the next few years, James Jnr. as he was called was growing into a lovely boy. Gentle like his father and with a love of music. Maria had told everyone who the father was and how it happened and how they were in fact married. James also had a lot of his mother in him. He could be fiery, emotional and he was ambitious. At school he excelled himself, and when he was only ten years old; there was no doubt in his mind that he would go to university. He stated it often and confidently.

Meanwhile, the business was going from strength to strength. They had expanded to two shops and the collection side of the business had multiplied. Maria had always insisted no matter how rich they became she wanted to keep the market stalls. She couldn't give them up. They were to her the very beginning and to truly succeed. You never forget.

Maria now lived in a large house with beautiful gardens and a fancy car. James attended a private school and she had a woman who cleaned for her. Not far away lived Tim and Laura, together with their children. They now had four, Paul, Emma, Sam and Ben. Ada had refused to move but did spend a lot of time visiting and staying over with Maria.

It had been thirteen years since she had seen David and though he was a distant memory she thought of him often.

Two children who loved each other was how she remembered
the past. But remember she did, often when out walking she
would see someone who looked like him and her heart would
skip a beat. She no longer felt any anger now though, she
accepted he did love her but circumstances had made it such
that it could never be.

She did have James, and for that she was so grateful. He
made her feel like a real person. She loved him so much it
almost hurt. She thought her life was almost complete. Maria
had always spoken highly of his father to James Jnr, of how he
had gone to America to find' fame and fortune' as he so loved
to say. He had written when he had arrived, giving Maria a
return address. At first she didn't know whether to tell him
about James Jnr. Not because she didn't want him to know,
she just didn't want him to feel under any obligation to leave
America and come back.

In the end she did tell him and he wrote the most
wonderful letters to herself and to James. Maria had placed
them all together in a box so that he could read them when he
was older. He was still waiting for fame and fortune, but
James said he was happy and loved America and had a special
friend. Maria was so glad for him.

It was in the winter of 1969 when the letter came. The
letter that broke her heart as she remembered all the
wonderful days they had spent together, and now he was
saying she may never see him again. James said he hadn't
wanted her to worry as there was nothing she could do for
him. Except he said," love my son for me and tell him how
very proud I am of his mother." Maria couldn't help it she
cried for days, wanted to go to him but he had begged her not
to.

"Remember me as I was my sweet innocent love. The doctors don't really understand this illness I have and as yet there is no effective medication available. I have had it for many years my darling Maria, that's why I wouldn't let you come over to see me. That is also the reason I never came to see my son. I hope you will both forgive me, I have and always will, love you both."

She couldn't continue it hurt her so much, she was already missing him and that was just by him saying remember me. He thanked her for giving him a son, said he was the proudest and happiest man ever. She really wanted to go to him more than anything in the world, he couldn't go not without her seeing him. But he made her promise, and she respected him too much to go against his last wishes.

That was the last time she heard from James. The next letter she received from America was to inform her of his death. He died leaving her the sole rights of his music and the house in which he had lived. There was also another letter from someone called Tony, he had been living at the house for five years and was still actively trying to get James recognised as a gifted musician.

"I realise you will probably sell the property, but could I continue acting as his agent? To me he was the most gifted musician there has been in a long time. He deserves to be recognised"

Reading the letter Maria could feel his sadness, and his loss, and knew there was a special love between them. She could feel it and somehow it made her feel happier knowing James had had someone to love him, and be with him until the end. Maria decided to let Tony carry on doing what he was doing and to continue living in the house, which he had shared with

James.

Tony became a close friend. His letters were personal and natural. He felt close to Maria because he knew they had both loved and shared the loss of one close to the heart. He was an avid writer who informed her of everything in the music business, and what he was doing. It was as if they were both reliving some part of James's life that each had had, and it was such a nice feeling. She was happy and enjoyed the closeness that had formed between them. To Maria it was as if her family had grown and she had become the centre of so much love and happiness. Even Cathy was now writing long letters, telling all about her new life.

Cathy told Maria how she had met a boy and loved him deeply. He was a farmer from the adjoining land to her grandfathers. She went into great detail about him. His name was Gordon Roberts and he had brown sandy hair, green eyes with the longest dark lashes and the most wonderful smile. Maria got the impression Cathy was well and truly besotted.

"Just hope your love life is better than mine," she thought wistfully.

Maria wrote a nice long letter back, wishing her all the love and happiness she so deserved, and hoped her future would be bright, and that Gordon sounded like a really nice person.

Chapter Twenty Three.

It was raining, Maria feeling a little nostalgic decided to get a cab and then walk the last couple of miles which would take her past the first stall she had worked on, before continuing onto her own stalls.

"Well, well what have we here, don't tell me you are slumming."

Maria stopped in her tracks, her brain going into overdrive as she recognised the voice. Slowly she turned, it was Michael. She couldn't help but notice he was looking even better than she remembered. Her heart raced so fast she was convinced he would notice, but her voice gave nothing away as she said quietly.

"Hello Michael."

"'Hello Michael',' is that all you have to say?"

Maria remained silent as she tried to figure out what was to do with him.

"I never thought the day would come when the bitch from hell, had nothing to say."

"Still as nice as ever I see."

"My father died, did you know? Oh sorry, of course you

did, seeing as how it was you who killed him."

"And how do you make that out?" Maria was confused.

"I can't believe you have forgotten. Is life so meaningless to you. It was you who put a curse on a superstitious old man. He died six months later."

"Michael, I have no idea what you are talking about, and I don't care."

"Typical! Just pretend it never happened."

"Well he wasn't exactly an asset to the human race was he? Now if you'll excuse me," she said as he barred her way.

"You really don't know do you? It was you."

"Michael I haven't seen you for over six years, spoken to you for ten years. What is your problem?"

"You bought his business for next to nothing, after you cursed him."

Realisation dawned on Maria. She had had a conversation with his father.

"I remember he tried to stop one of the main suppliers of Angora sweaters, from working with me. I called him a mean old man. He said I was evil."

"And then what?" Michael asked.

"I said it was him who was evil, and before the year was out every bad thing he had ever done, would come back to haunt him."

"Yeh, well it killed him. His mind went, said demons had possessed him. Said it was you who sent them."

"I can't help you there, they were his own demons."

"Don't you care?" Michael asked.

"Why should I, he meant nothing to me."

"You really are a bitch." He said.

"And you were always a bastard."

The strength of her words stunned him. He stared silently into her eyes and became aware the girl he once knew was no longer there.

"Come on," she said, "accept what you are, then move on. Life is too short."

He remained quiet, looking at the new Maria he felt awkward, almost intimidated, she appeared to be strong and in control. He viewed her with a new admiration.

"Look, do you want a drink? I'm buying," she said impulsively.

"Generous to a fault and still fancying me," he smiled; happy she had broken the cold atmosphere.

"No I am getting wet, and this is not the nicest place to go into on your own."

"For old time's sake," he laughed.

"I don't think so," Maria answered, but she was enjoying the banter, and she wanted to know if the rumours about him were true. Apparently he was a reformed character.

After they had bought their drinks, they sat in front of the window. Through the rain Maria saw that same stall that she had been so happy working on all those years ago when she was just a child.

"A life time ago," she reflected to herself, "but where is life taking that child now?" she pondered.

She had more money than she could spend, a wonderful son and friends that were like a family. Even Cathy had started to write and sounded like the sister she had always wanted. And yet she knew there was still something missing in her life. She wanted the love of her real family, her real mother but felt as though they were no longer part of her. It was as if it had all been a terrible mistake and that she wasn't really a part of them.

Then she turned to Michael.

"What am I doing sitting here with you?"

"I have no idea, and I really don't want to analyse it." He said.

"No?"

"No"

They both slipped into an easy silence each remembering the good times. Then Maria's face creased as the bad times broke through.

"We can't move on in our respective lives if we don't sort out the past," Michael said.

Maria nodded.

"I'm sorry Maria," he said after what seemed like an eternity. "I'm sorry for everything, but it's you I have to thank for helping me to change."

"How do you make that out?"

"All my life I wasn't good enough. My father never failed to tell me at every possible opportunity. I felt inferior at school, and totally inadequate at business. He bought me the stall and told me how to run it, like it was a multi-million pound conglomerate."

"Why didn't you leave?"

"Because by the time I was ten, I believed everything he told me. It was at a party, he organised one every year and said I could invite any one I liked. Then in front of everyone he told me I didn't even know how to play without my friends showing me. And that I would never become anything in life.

"He was a very cruel man." Maria said.

"Yes I suppose, but after that I did everything he told me. Hoping one day he would be proud of me."

"And was he?"

"No, he wasn't and never would be, I know that now."

"How is that?"

"After he died, I found out he wasn't really my father. He had hated me since the day I was born. He even tried to cut me out of his will."

"Did he succeed?"

"Apparently the money came from my mother's side of the family and wasn't his to leave to anyone."

"So you did inherit?"

"There wasn't much left after you had finished with it," he said. "Don't worry, I don't blame you, I wish I had half the strength you have." Taking Maria's hand, Michael looked tenderly into her eyes.

"I did love you, you know."

She pulled her hand away, he had broken the spell. Up until that moment she was starting to feel sorry for him.

"Please Maria, let me explain, the only time I felt important was when I was with a young girl. I never had the confidence to ask anyone out of my own age. But once by accident I took out a pretty little redhead. She was my first date, I never thought to ask her how old she was, and I was just too excited at going out with a girl. I was twenty and a virgin, she made me feel important. It was her, even though she said she was sixteen. She educated me on how to be a good lover. It didn't last long but after that I soon realised all the young girls would look up to me and respect me."

"Respect you!"

"I know, it sounds incredulous, like I am making excuses, but that was how it was. And then when they got a bit older I had to finish before they found out I was just a fraud and couldn't do anything."

As Maria listened and watched him, he did seem genuine.

"And now?" she ventured.

"After my father died, life took on a different meaning. There was no one continually berating me for being a failure and I started to feel stronger. I opened up a stall with my own money and bought what I wanted. But the best feeling was when I plucked up the courage to ask this gorgeous barmaid who worked at the 'Flat Iron Pub' to come out with me. She accepted and we had the most fantastic time for almost a year."

"A year?" she said with mock incredulity.

"Yeah, a full year. Then there was no holding me. I no longer needed to impress little girls, which, by the way. I'm greatly ashamed of now. I could have fully fledged women."

Maria listened, keeping an open mind. She had heard too many stories in her life and had become quite cynical as to the truth of many. Though she hoped that this was one occasion where she really could believe. He seemed so genuinely sorry for what he had done.

"The only exception Maria was you," he said in earnest.

"Flattery will get you nowhere."

"No, really, you were never a child were you. Young maybe but not childish. Remember our Tuesday afternoons, we couldn't fake that Maria. It was real. I was just frightened you would leave me eventually and, as it happens, you did.

"For family reasons Michael, nothing else."

"I still think of you."

"Don't you go giving me that blarney, remember I know you."

"Maria at least we can be friends. Ten years is a long time to miss someone."

"All we had Michael, on reflection, was sex."

"It was good though, wasn't it?"

She smiled, she couldn't help it. It was good to be talking again, and if she was really truthful to herself, she had to admit she had missed that intimate bodily contact.

"Oh sack it," she said aloud.

"What?" he asked puzzled.

She couldn't tell him that she hadn't had sex for over ten years and that that was only the once. And yes, her natural urges were gaining strength. But she was too frightened to go into any kind of relationship. She had never had one that lasted and sometimes thought life had cheated her.

"Michael," she said, "let's meet again, on Tuesday."

"Honest?" He asked with incredibility.

"I don't want you Michael, I just need your body." She laughed.

"Maria I love you."

Chapter Twenty Four.

It was 1976 and James, now a young man of nineteen was enjoying being a student. Like his father he had a great love of music and wanted to be a teacher. His mother was thankful he didn't feel the need to seek fame and fortune, but then there was nothing he couldn't have. His nature was a strong mixture of both his parents, philosophical, gentle and loving. He was also strong and stood his ground when there was any misdemeanour or wrong doing. He couldn't tolerate unfairness, and was also on hand to help anyone out.

Business was good, profits were rising and life in general was going along quite well. Tim and Laura were expecting their first grandchild. Emma was positively blooming and had the adoration of a very wonderful husband who she loved very much. They were, Maria felt, the most perfect family she had ever known. They still loved each other, had planned children together and were delighted to make them the centre of their life.

However, Maria was beginning to feel bored. Life held no challenges for her. Her son was an absolute star in her eyes. She couldn't have asked for a nicer child, he was well mannered and intelligent, considerate and loving. He was she had to admit, his father's son most of the time. But in general he really didn't need her very much now, he was finding his own life, and she respected that. He in turn respected his mother's private life. Which as a general rule was very quiet, except for the occasional weekends away with Michael.

Michael had become a good friend and someone Maria could relate to. She had known him through the years of poverty and innocence and he was, she decided, part of her life. Now, in her world of affluence, he was her reminder of what life was really like for most people. As she remembered her nights of passion, she had to admit that he had been true to her now for many years and he professed undying love. Maria believed him, but couldn't respond. Something inside her still wouldn't let go, she couldn't love.

James was happy, so Maria was happy. He had made a new friend at college who was an orphan and was working his way through college.

"He is just the opposite of what I am mother, but we just seemed to click. I'm doing Music, he's doing Business Studies. I enjoy life, he just works."

Maria smiled, she was so proud of him. For all his wealthy lifestyle there was no difference in the way he treated people. In fact he seemed to favour the hard working, poor students more.

"Is it alright if I invite him home for the summer holidays. That is, if I can persuade him to take time off from work?"

"Do you think he will?"

"Well he has to leave the accommodation he's in, and if he doesn't have to pay for the next room until the start of the next term he won't have to worry about rent, and we do get on awfully well."

"You seem to have it all worked out."

"Yes, I do hope he comes mother, you will like him I'm
sure of that. His name is David, he's Jewish."

Maria felt her heart take a flutter, even now after all these
years she missed her David. That was how she thought of him
now, her David, who she knew she would never see again. It
was a quiet feeling inside her, which told her he was gone. But
she still clung to hope, it was as if some part of her life was
always to be entwined with his. And that feeling never left.

All night Maria tossed and turned, but sleep wouldn't
come. Something somewhere in her mind was disturbing her,
what, she didn't know. Looking at herself in the mirror she
had to admit that no amount of makeup was going to help
her, she looked terrible. And today was the day James was
bringing his friend home, she so wanted to make a good
impression and welcome him for her son's sake. He had never
really asked her to do anything for him before, so she knew
whoever this friend was, her son thought a lot of him.

Standing in front of the mirror, putting on a touch of
lipstick and running a comb through her hair, she stopped to
study her reflection. It was a different face from that of years
ago, she mused. Her long dark hair had become 'modern and
sophisticated', she thought to herself as she looked at the
short bob-cut. The colour had highlights running through it
giving it a lift so that it no longer looked black.

"I am 36 years old, have everything most people would
want, so why do I feel sad?" she pondered.

There had always been a kind of emptiness, in Maria; it was
only now she had started to question why.

A car could be heard drawing up; Maria looked out of her bedroom window. She was dressed nicely, she knew that, but she still felt on edge. James had arrived, she watched and her heart, as always, filled with love and pride when she saw him. Even now, after all these years she still found it hard to believe that he was her son. She loved him so much, there was nothing she wouldn't so for him. And yet he was so unaffected by life.

His friend stepped out from the car and Maria all but fainted. He was David re-incarnated, even from where she stood she could see the resemblance. The same build, same colouring, even the same walk, David had a kind of lilt to the left and this friend of James had exactly the same.

Maria clung to the chair, she needed to steady herself. Her mind was playing tricks she knew underneath somehow she was never going to see David again. So why was she imagining him being down stairs with her son. But then her mind made her see how stupid she was being. James's friend whoever he was, looked the image of David, but that was nearly twenty years ago. The David of today would look nothing like the lad downstairs.

Taking herself in control she put a smile on her face and went down to welcome her son, and his friend. Maria was visibly shaken as she shook hands with him. There was no getting away from it, he was the image of 'her' David.

As the night wore on, Maria relaxed. They had had a delicious meal, James was on top form, talking laughing making David feel at home. She admired her son very much, but that evening her attention was focussed on David.

He told her how his mother had died in childbirth and his

father had brought him up alone. His father had been called David, and was a man who fought hard for the Jewish people. He worked tirelessly for the cause and for his people. Until one fateful day, he had been caught in a cross fire. This took place in Israel when David had been on patrol in the Golan Heights, he had died instantly. Long before he died he had always made his wishes known. He wanted David to come to England and have an education. A small amount of money had been left for him to help achieve this.

Maria desperately tried to control her emotions as he spoke in detail about his father and the life he led, but also the life he had left behind in England. The more he spoke, the more she realised that this was in fact David's son. She was convinced that fate had brought them together for a reason.

The following day found Maria sitting beside the lake in Heaton Park. It was the exact same place she had sat with David, when they had almost kissed and when she thought her heart would stop. Today she sat alone, her eyes resting on the cool water, and the many wonderful rhododendron bushes that had given them so much delight and happiness that day.

"They might have been hard times David, but we had some good times didn't we?" she whispered. "And don't worry, I will look after your son like he was my very own."

Suddenly she felt happy, there was a lightness in her step she hadn't felt for a long time. But it was the warm feeling she had, the feeling that David was at last with her. He had come to her when he needed help for his son. He trusted her to look after him and she knew underneath David really had loved her.

Chapter Twenty Five.

The music business she had invested in was going well. But the last phone call made her feel apprehensive. James had written a song she treasured and kept for herself. It was personal and she wanted to keep it like that. But Tony was begging her to let him release it on the next album. He had found a recording locked away, "James must have done it just before he died," Tony said. "It's fantastic, the best he's ever done and would give him the recognition he so desperately craved when he was alive". Maria was torn, she hadn't discussed it with her son because she knew it had to be her decision. She wanted James to rest in peace, in the knowledge his music would be enjoyed the world over. In her heart she knew what she had to do. It had been his dream. She would go to America. If her song could make his dream come true, then she had no choice. James had wanted nothing more than to bring peace and happiness to the world. As much as the song had been hers for so long, it had brought so much comfort to her and she had come to think of it as her own little bit of private happiness, she knew she had to let it go, to share it with the world, it was what he would have wanted.

Maria was away for two weeks, but in that time she had authorised the release of the record James had written for her. The title was 'Whispers of Love'

"That is so like him." she had said when she heard the title. He used to whisper lovely words of love.

The song had brought her a new kind of strength, and a love she would never forget. James had given her the knowledge of how to deal with life. That had been his legacy to her, and she loved him dearly for it.

While in America, Maria studied the market. She knew that whatever America did now, Britain would do tomorrow. And America was selling films to the ordinary household. No longer did they have to go to the drive-in to watch a movie, they could do it in the comfort of their own home by video.

Maria's business brain took over. She could see the potential, and knew that this was big. She wasn't interested in the actual video player but she realised that there was definitely money to be made in supplying the films for rental. Already her mind was working overtime, she loved a new challenge and this was it.

Tim was happy, he didn't really want to change his life. Business was good and he loved what he was doing.

"Maria" he said, "I knew in time you would want a fresh challenge."

"You don't mind?"

"No I really don't mind."

"Tim you have to be one of the nicest people I know."

Tim laughed. "Not really, I knew this day would come, so I have been saving. Knowing when you did want to sell I could buy you out." He said it like it was the most natural thing in the world.

This time it was Maria who laughed.

"No wonder I always had faith in you." Well, now she had the money, but not the partner.

After giving it a lot of thought, Maria consulted James on her new idea. He was wholeheartedly in agreement and couldn't wait for her to tell David.

David sat almost speechless.

"Why?" he said in amazement.

"Let's just say you remind me of someone I once knew many years ago. It was someone who taught me how to live and exist, in a world when I was just a child."

"There has to be more to it than that surely?" David asked, still in shock at the deal he had just been offered.

"Of course, I'm a business woman. This is a new adventure and I need someone with ambition, a hunger to succeed. Plus you have the business acumen that's needed. You are about to qualify in business management and accountancy, aren't you?"

"Yes."

"And you want to fulfil your father's wishes, so what more do I need to know?"

"This is all true, but twenty per cent of the business plus a salary." David was still in shock.

"Well unless you work hard that twenty per cent will mean nothing."

Maria loved the way he was trying to understand her generosity.

"Well what do you say?" she said.

"I say in twelve months the business will be one of the most successful in the country."

"Now that's what I like to hear." She said laughing, and as her eyes looked into his she saw David, and that same warm feeling spread over her once again. She might not have had his presence but she knew she had, had some of his love. He had proved it by sending his son to her. His son being here in her house with James, made her realise this was in some way David's way of giving her the one thing she had always wanted and needed, and that was to have been part of his life. And when the time came she would tell his son.

The radio played the song that had climbed into the top ten in England and top three in America.

'Whispers of Love' was a huge success and it coincided with the official forming of the company. Maria was happy in a deep rooted way. It was as though her loves of the past had come together to bring her peace and to help her embrace the future with an open heart.

Except there was one dark cloud on the horizon, and that was her family. Cathy wrote often. She had married and surprised Maria by naming her first child after her. John also wrote, but the last letter had informed her that her grandfather was ill and her father had returned. She couldn't help it, all the old feelings of hate which she had fought hard to dispel, came flooding back.

Maria knew if she was to truly move on as James had said, she had to do something she could barely even contemplate.

"You have to face life." He had said. And she knew the part of her life that she had not been able to come to terms with, was her father. She had hidden from it far too long, and as her hands covered her face in anguish she knew the time had come. She had to deal with it.

Packing a few things, Maria felt apprehensive. Her life should be happy; everything she had ever wanted was hers.

"So why do I have to go?" she asked herself as she stopped and stared deep into the mirror.

But it wasn't the smart sophisticated Maria who stared back; it was the frightened child with the wild eyes and dirty face. A child who shouted at the world and knew nothing about childhood, who had been used and abused and had never known how to laugh or play. Tears welled up into Maria's eyes as she remembered how it was, always to be hungry and feel the pain of her younger brother and sister, to watch her mother's life waste away, see her living in a world of isolation within her own mind, and then she remembered the pain of pure hate, of dreams awash in frightening scenes of fire and cruelty and the face of her father. And then he was gone. None of this she understood.

Maria turned to wipe a tear from her cheek, unable to look

any more because she knew, underneath, she would always be that little girl until she put all her ghosts away. It was her father, he was the only one she had never been able to forgive, just thinking about him hurt, he was like something ugly inside that she couldn't get rid of.

That frightened little girl was still there and she couldn't understand why after all these years she was so very afraid of him. There had to be a reason, but no matter how hard she tried, she couldn't find it. Pulling herself up Maria faced the mirror once more.

"David is part of my life, he sent me his son. Michael has changed. James gave me more than I could wish for, so why am I letting someone who calls himself my father spoil my happiness? I can't do it anymore," Tears fell fast and furious as she lost control of her emotions. She cried aloud, and her heart was at breaking point as the pain of ignorance overwhelmed her.

"I have to go, I know that. But am I strong enough?" The thoughts ran around her head until it hurt. "I can't pretend anymore," she whispered as the need to understand wouldn't go away.

So many unanswered questions which had plagued her now needed resolving. It was time. She had to be strong. Whatever it was that she feared had to be dealt with, she couldn't live any longer under the cloud of hate and the not knowing what had actually happened all those years ago. What had he done, that could give her such deep frightening nightmares about things that seemed unreal, and the burning fire that was ever present...

Meanwhile, up in Scotland, the summer was hot,

grandfather was feeling better and Ailsa was basking in the love of her new found relationship with her husband. Life was to all intents just perfect. Anton knew Ailsa's father didn't have very long to live and he had overwhelmed her mother with charm and compliments and she was now a great fan of his. Forgotten was the past, they now played the respectable united family. Anton preened himself on being able to get them not only to forgive him but to embrace him and welcome him into their home.

Ailsa didn't really understanding what he was saying, but he was nice and said nice things and that was all that mattered to her.

"We belong together" he smiled pulling her closer as he looked up towards the ceiling from his large comfortable bed. "Aye it's a grand house" he thought to himself.

Chapter Twenty Six.

Cathy was happy. She had a husband who adored her, and a home she positively glowed in. Gordon was a farmer, and by her own admission he was her best friend as well as her husband. He had helped her to grow up and understand a lot of the things that had gone on in her life. Having known her grandparents for most of his life, he knew what they were capable of and helped Cathy to see how hard it must have been for Maria. Today though she was apprehensive, as much as she wanted to see Maria, she was frightened. Frightened for Maria, she didn't want any of the hate and ill feelings to be hurled at her any more. And she knew her father would start on Maria as soon as he saw her.

John arrived, and became immediately aware of the grief his sister was feeling. At first he thought something was terribly wrong. John ran the Estate, lived up in the big house and loved his work. He wasn't married but was in a serious relationship with Morag who came from Nairn. He was comfortable with life and looked forward to the future.

"What's wrong?" he asked tenderly knowing how sensitive his sister was.

"I had a letter from Maria. She says she is coming up to visit but I am worried."

"Why? If you are thinking of them up there stop worrying. Maria can handle anything they throw at her."

Cathy became quiet as she remembered, "I still miss her

John, even after all these years. And I still think the past haunts our Maria"

"You may be right Cathy, but let's hope this visit will help to put the past where it belongs and we can all move on, if only for her sake. Mind you I wouldn't hold my breath. It's worse now than ever. Grandfather still blames her for being born. Mother isn't sure what reality is and our dear father is quite happy to blame everyone except himself. But the worst thing is, he's feeding grandmother's hate towards Maria."

"It's not good, is it John?"

"No, and they refuse to listen to anything I have to say."

Cathy nodded as if in agreement but her mind couldn't rationalise the coincidence of her coming up to visit after all these years. Not now that her father had reappeared on the scene, taken up residence and acted like he'd done nothing wrong.

"How do you think they will react up there, when they find out she is back?"

"Well I wouldn't say she is back Cathy, she is only coming for a visit, but I know what you mean. But as for them up there, I don't know how they will react. They think everything is wonderful and would have been like that years ago except......

"I know, except for Maria. How can they blame her after what they've done, it just doesn't seem right."

168

"It makes them feel better shifting the blame, removes the guilt."

"I know you love the land John, but how do you live with them?"

"Simple, I never see them."

Chapter Twenty Seven.

James Fleming Snr. lay propped up on pillows. His once large frame seemed to have shrunk and his face was grey with a tinge of blue around his lips. As he looked at her, a slight smile appeared, he was tired, very tired but he knew he only had this one chance of finding out the truth.

"Hello my dear," he said sadly, "please come closer," his voice barely audible.

Maria looked at this frail old man and her heart went out to him. They had never met, and he didn't know who she was or who she was related to. But Maria could see her James in the softness of his eyes.

"Thank you so much for coming, tell me, was he happy? Did he hate me?" There were tears in his eyes as he waited for her reply, convinced his only grandson must have hated him for being weak, and not standing by him.

"James couldn't hate anyone sir. He was the most loving gentle man I have ever known. He said he was like you and that he couldn't have been happier. You were everything to him. He knew his parents through your memories and he loved you for that."

"Did he forgive me?"

"Yes, he said his life was full of love and he owed everything to you. He said it wasn't your fault you didn't understand, he didn't understand himself. He always loved you." She said gently, but with a sincerity he knew could only be true.

"Thank you, thank you." He held out his hand and Maria felt his love, and also his sadness.

"The last few years we spent together they were........

"They were good," she interrupted "you have no need to reproach yourself he understood how it was for you."

"He forgave me?"

"Yes he forgave you, like he forgave me, he loved us both."

"Is it true I have a great grandson?"

"Yes" she whispered, aware he was becoming very tired. "His name is James."

"You have made an old man very happy," he said weakly, then smiling he repeated, "James."

And there still holding her hand he died. Maria didn't move, overcome with emotion she felt a kind of love for this old man who still had a smile on his face, and was sorry she had never got to know him. She was happy that she had helped him to die in peace, knowing his grandson bore him no malice. But she was also sad that his great grandson, her James, had never had the opportunity to know him.

"Why is it only when we are near death, that we reflect on life and realise what is important?" she asked herself.

Chapter Twenty Eight.

The two sisters embraced each other with a passion none of them expected. Cathy was crying, she was so happy to see her, and Maria couldn't help her own tears from coming. How good it felt to be with her sister again. She was overwhelmed, she hadn't really known what to expect. Half of her was afraid that time would have drawn them apart or her mother would have influenced Cathy, but no, it was as she hoped it would be, the old familiarity of childhood was still there, and she hugged Cathy tightly as though she would never let go. Cathy also was overcome with emotion, not so much in seeing her but feeling her holding her so close.

Cathy had always wanted to be loved when she was a child, it was only as she matured she realised how much Maria must have loved her to do what she had done. 'You don't know that, though, when you're young, you just want someone to hug you and say nice things' thought Cathy. Maria was never demonstrative, Cathy only realised as she got older that her sister probably didn't know how to show affection. After all, she had never had anyone to show her any kind of affection. To Cathy she had just been her big sister who looked after them, she now realised how young Maria had been, and fervently hoped she had found happiness in her adult life.

It was only when she herself was married and had children of her own that Cathy started looking at life differently. It was then she realised just how badly Maria had been treated. Her mother was weak and selfish, her grandparents wanted to control everything and discarded anyone or anything they thought wasn't up to their standards. They were snobbish in a most profound and selfish way. Maria was a reminder of what their daughter had done, and they didn't like it, so they banished her from their thoughts and heaped all the blame and unhappiness that had befallen them onto her. As far as they were concerned, she didn't belong with them, and they had no intention of ever having her in their home. On the other hand, Anton had been welcomed back because he gave Ailsa respectability and he no longer looked so foreign, now that he was grey. Anton dreamed of the day when Ailsa's father passed away and then he would be in complete control of everything. He could only imagine what kind of wealth there was. The land, the big house the smaller farmhouses. How happy he felt. He smiled to himself as he tried to think what kind of money would be in the bank, and like a true hypocrite he thanked God for making him happy and giving him so much. Sometimes he felt sorry for Maria, but that was quickly replaced by self-preservation. If everyone wanted to blame her, that was fine by him. He wasn't going to upset anybody at this present time, too much was at stake.

"Besides, she can take it." he concluded selfishly

Chapter Twenty Nine.

It was a beautiful morning, the sun was rising up over the mountains, the sky was a lovely shade of pale blue and there wasn't a cloud in sight. A soft breeze filtered through the window, Maria stood filling her lungs with the crisp fresh air she only encountered in the Scottish Highlands, and the old familiar scent of the hills made her remember James. She missed him, she missed the Highlands. There could be was no other place in the whole world she thought, to compare it with. In all directions from her window she could see the snow-capped mountains, the trees the rugged hills where she knew the deer would be resting. The colours of the heather were more beautiful than ever, the browns and yellows mixed happily together with the vibrant purple giving the earth a warm inviting feel to it. Only the Scottish heather could live in harmony with such strong forces of nature she remembered. Her eyes rested in the far distance, she was sure she could see James's cottage. She had to go.

"Cathy," she said, "I'm going out for a walk, I won't be too long."

"Would you like me to come with you?"

"There is something I have to do, and I need to be alone, you don't mind do you?"

Cathy looked worried.

"Don't worry I'm not going up there, not yet anyway, no this is going to be pleasant. I know you should never go back to somewhere where you were happy, that it's never the same, but I disagree. Today I'm going to revisit the past, and I'm looking forward to it."

"I didn't even know you knew anybody up here, let alone experience any kind of happiness."

"One day when I'm ready I will tell you everything. You know I have always loved you I just find it hard to say. There was one short period in my life which I spent up there, on the mountain. And it gave me so much I really do want to share it with you. I learnt so much about life, Cathy, from someone who was very dear to me."

"Was?"

"Yes, I will tell you soon, but not just yet. There's something I have to do first."

Cathy had never seen Maria like this, she looked so tranquil and serene, she was remembering something really wonderful Cathy could tell, and was intrigued.

"I will tell you soon I promise," Maria smiled.

Whatever it was, Cathy realised it had played a major part in Maria's life.

As Maria sat quietly on the veranda overlooking the valley, watching the still waters of the Loch below, she was filled with a deep sense of peace. The sun shone brightly as it danced in and out of the tall Scottish Pine trees reflecting the true colours on the water. To Maria it was like a magnificent painting that had come to life.

"James," she said looking towards the sky, "no wonder you loved it here, it's perfect. I can feel you James, like when you used to say you could feel your parents. Now I know what you meant. Help me James to find the strength to deal with my parents and grandparents. I want to bring our son here, to feel the love you have for him. I'm sorry that I haven't brought him to you before now. I just want it to be a happy experience and until I sort out what's going on in my head about those in the big house, I can't do it. I need your strength James; I need to fully walk away from my 'brick wall' as you would say."

Maria sat quietly for a while, her mind empty, her breathing deep and even. The mountain air seeped through into her body, waking every part of her in a calm, relaxing way, making her whole countenance feel peaceful and strong. And she felt the nearness of her James.

"I am ready," she whispered into the breeze as she stood.

Chapter Thirty.

It was wonderful being there, sitting around the table sharing a meal

"Let's talk about your life?" she said looking at Cathy.

"I love my life," she said "Gordon is wonderful and the children bring me so much happiness. I'm lucky. We're not terribly wealthy, but neither do we have to worry about money."

"What about you John?"

"I'm still up there. I love my work, I practically run the whole estate now. The only thing is they will not pay me a decent wage, and if I want to get married, which I do, I will have to leave and find a job with more money." He sighed heavily, "It's a shame I love the land but I do need my own space, I want my own house and hopefully have gorgeous children like our Cathy," he said smiling looking over at her.

Cathy blushed with pride.

"What about you Maria?" John inquired knowingly.

"I'm doing alright," she smiled.

"You always say that," Cathy laughed, "yet my friend said she saw one of them fancy magazines when she was visiting her auntie in London. She said it had a picture of you in it, said you had won 'Businesswoman of the Year' award. She said it showed a photo of a grand house with its own lake, and one of them posh cars, a 'Rolls Royce'. She knew it was you because she had seen that photo you sent us last Christmas."

"We both knew it was you, Maria. We were so proud."

Maria looked from one to the other, they had turned out such nice people, there wasn't a jealous bone between them, they were just genuinely good honest hard working people.

"No, it's me that is overcome with pride." She said "and I mean that with all my heart, and yes, the time will come to tell you about my life, but that time isn't now."

They looked disappointed but accepted they would have to wait. As Maria enjoyed sitting there with John and Cathy and her family, she thought how normal and natural it all seemed. Yet it was the first time in her life she had ever done it. The food was excellent. Cathy had really turned into a wonderful housewife and mother. Gordon looked at his wife as she passed him the potatoes and Maria couldn't help but see the love and tenderness in his eyes. She was so happy for Cathy and yet a little sad also as she realised it was one of those things that had passed her by in life.

It was during the meal that Maria announced she was going up to the house the following day. Cathy and John, who had come over for dinner, felt the panic rising in them. They were afraid for Maria. Donald, Cathy's husband, who knew a little of what had gone on before, broke the silence.

"I'll drive you Maria."

Maria turned, grateful for his support.

"Me and Cathy, we'll come too" John said.

Cathy nodded. "Definitely "she said.

The children looked on in anticipation.

"You'll be at school." Cathy said smiling.

"Could we drive just half way?" Maria asked. "Only I think I'd like to walk a little."

"What, just like old times?" John smiled sadly. "Us three walking"

Morning came and with it a bright cheerful Maria, who wasn't going to think about them up in the big house until she had to. For now, she would just dismiss them from her mind, and enjoy the walk. Maria missed walking in the country, missed being able to go out without having to wear make-up or worry about how her hair looked or if her clothes were suitable.

Today, though, she felt free, the wind blew her hair wild and she didn't care. It had been a long time since she had felt this free. Inside she knew the day was here, the day when all her demons would take flight and leave her to live a normal life, to unravel the many paths of her pain.

A smile spread across her face as the realisation hit her; she really did feel as though she was about to gain her life back.

Whatever had happened to her in the past was about to be set free.

Turning her attention to John and Cathy she could hear them talking quietly together, their faces looking strained. Maria knew they were worried what kind of reception she was going to get, but she wasn't and she couldn't make them understand that.

"Some things never change, so you two just stop worrying. I know they don't want to meet me or even see me."

"Then why are you going?" John asked.

"You know they're just going to upset you." Cathy added.

"I know, but it's something I have to do, I'll explain later. It's to do with a brick wall." Then she laughed at the expressions on their faces.

There was something inside Maria that was buried so deep it couldn't be touched. Something that had plagued her for as long as she could remember, but as to why, she didn't know. The nightmares, the tears and the fear, they wouldn't go away, and she had a nagging feeling that it all had something to do with her father. Because, she rationalised, there had to be a reason why she felt the way she did about him. He had left them, and she had resented him for that, but what she felt was so strong it couldn't be justified. And that confused her, and strengthened the feeling that something terrible had happened and that he was involved. Not knowing or understanding distressed her. She desperately needed to sort her mind out.

As her steps quickened, her mind began to rationalise that maybe today when they met it would all come tumbling back. The three of them made their way through the garden, Gordon stayed behind understanding how they may need some privacy. As they approached the house they heard his voice, loud and angry, he was in the garden to the right beside the rose bushes.

"What are you doing here?" Anton hissed as he stared at Maria. He slowly walked over to the bench where some plants and garden tools lay, his arrogance plain for all to see. Smiling, he picked up a sharp knife, his intention being to intimidate them. But as he turned he realised something was wrong.

The blood had drained from Maria and her face was now white, her eyes wide and staring. She stood like a statue as if in a trance.

Suddenly Anton had a flashback to when Maria was a child, and slowly it came back to him as he remembered. She had looked exactly like that on that fateful night so long ago. A shiver ran down his back, he needed her to go, to leave. He wanted rid of her. He was frightened.

"Why the hell did you come back?"

She didn't answer, her eyes silently bore into his, unnerving him even more.

John looked at Cathy in bewilderment.

"What is going on?" he whispered.

Cathy shrugged. Her father was hostile and threatening and yet he also appeared to be in deep shock. What really confused them though was the fact he was frightened. His fear could be felt in the air. It was all around them, but why? And what had it to do with Maria?

Maria continued to stand transfixed, her mind was opening, memories, came flooding back. Back to the night her horrors had begun. Horrors so bad her young mind had blocked them out.

Her father was now perspiring as he also remembered, and suddenly he was terrified. His heart was beating wildly and his head felt as though it would explode. The pain was intense.

"Go," he said "please go," but as he lifted his hand, unaware he was still holding the knife, Maria screamed. Something deep inside her snapped. She flew at him, her nails tearing at his face and all the time screaming abuse. She was like a mad woman. Anton fell to the ground and John had to pull her off him. He thought she was going to kill him.

Then, just as suddenly as her outburst had started, she became deathly quiet. She hated him, it was written on her face for all to see. But the pain was also there.

"You were so drunk you could hardly stand," she said in a whisper, "but still you carried on as she screamed louder and louder. You wouldn't stop." The anguish in her voice was heart-breaking. Tears rolled down her face silently.

Her father tried to move, he couldn't take any more, he didn't want to remember. It was the knife, the knife had opened the door to his mind as it had to Maria's, he looked down on it as he realised Maria's eyes were transfixed. And then he knew. He could feel the real pain of fear as he realised she had at last remembered, and there was nothing he could do.

Her face was as cold as granite but her voice was husky with raw emotion, she spoke with a controlled quietness that seemed unreal.

"You had a knife that night didn't you? You stifled her screams as you cut into her a little at a time until she passed out." Maria paused unable to go on as the full horror of the night invaded her mind. "And then you saw me, I had come out to try and help Ma. Instead you laughed and grabbed me, you tore off my clothes and when Ma came round you told her terrible things about what you had done to me."

"Please Maria, no more" he pleaded as he looked at the horror and disgust on the faces of his other children.

"Every day, you said, every single day of her life she would look at me and see you." Maria was talking but it was as if she was reliving something so terrible she couldn't quite believe it.

"I remember the knife it was cold to my face as you taunted Ma. 'Should I cut it off?' you said. 'Should I take her face away, then she can't remind you.'"

Anton paled, his heart pounded like it had never done before, he felt out of control. Then the pain came. Like a vice that gripped without mercy his hand clutched his chest as he fell to the ground. But no one came to his aid.

The past blinded him as his body shook in pain. Maria stood over him and he remembered that night so very long ago. He had set fire to her, he had wanted to destroy her. Instead it had been himself, who had recoiled in fear. She was the devil, she should have died. He remembered her image in the glow of the fire as the darkness overcame him. Her eyes had been large and bright just as they were now. Deep piecing menacing eyes, with hair that moved in the wind, except that night there had been no wind, and he knew, he had felt it, she was possessed. And as the alcohol took over his brain on that fateful night he remembered collapsing to the ground. His last conscious thoughts before he passed out were of devils surrounding him, and his daughter standing alone unblinking. She was on fire, but wasn't burning.

As his memories haunted him, every part of his body was crying out in pain as he lay there upon the ground.

"Please stop," he begged.

But it was too late, what had been locked away all these years now came flooding out.

"No wonder she hates him." Cathy whispered quietly.

"It was you "Maria said. "You took away Ma's life in that instant. Then, when you woke, you left like the coward you are, leaving us with nothing. It was after that night Ma became depressed, but now I understand. It wasn't depression. She couldn't cope with what she'd seen and so she became a child again. Her mind blanked everything out and she became trapped in her childhood world. That's why she didn't understand that she was a mother herself and had children. You made her the way she is," Maria said. "You took away her life."

"No," he said, feeling the hate he had for his daughter return, even as he lay there in pain he thought only of the money he now had because he was back with Ailsa. There was no way he was going to lose it because of her.

"You can't blame me," he whispered weakly. "You should have stayed in bed. If you had she wouldn't have got hurt. It's your fault, always has been. And the hate in his eyes shone through deep and smouldering.

Maria felt the life in her body slip away, never had she felt this way. All the pain and heartache she had endured had never made her feel this bad. She stared at him in shock. John and Cathy couldn't believe their ears. Even now, lying on the ground in pain, he refused to acknowledge he had done anything wrong. He was still trying to shift the blame.

"Why?" John asked in disbelief. "Why are you like this?

But Anton could no longer speak as he clutched his chest in pain, his breathing became laboured, but still everyone stood by, just staring at him in shock.

"Help me please" he whispered.

No one moved.

"I am going back" Maria said quietly, "I have to think, I need time." But underneath she felt as though her heart was broken.

Chapter Thirty One.

Maria needed to go home, to feel love from her own son who she was missing so very much. Inside the pain wouldn't go away, she was hurting. His words pounded away inside her, she couldn't escape them.

As she quietly packed to return home she felt drained, as though her spirit had left her. Her thoughts tormented her. Was it all her fault? Would her mother have been alright if she hadn't gone out on that fateful night? But she couldn't ignore the screams could she? He was killing her mother, at least she thought he was, but now she didn't know. Maria thought she was helping her, she was crying, she could still hear the screams in her nightmares.

Maria couldn't take it anymore, she was tired and felt as though her insides had crumbled. How could she live with herself knowing it might have been her fault, they had always blamed her and now she had to face the truth?

"Were they right?"

Maria had thought that this was going to be the chance to move forward, to reclaim her life, but it had all gone wrong. Yes, she now knew her nightmares, except for the fire. She still didn't understand why she should keep thinking of a fire. At least now she knew how cruel her father was. But she didn't feel any kind of peace within herself. She felt as though she had failed once again.

James placed the receiver slowly down.

"What is it? I can tell by your face something is wrong."

"Mother's on her way home sounds very depressed, said she needs to talk."

"I would never have put your mother down as someone who would give in to depression. She always seems so strong. I didn't think it was in her nature."

"You know David I've never been to Scotland. Whenever it's come up in conversation she always looks sad. Yet she says she has never been happier than when she was up there with my father."

"It must be something very deep then. My father was the same. I always felt as though he wasn't telling me everything."

"I know what you mean. That's exactly how I feel about my mother."

"I never asked my father. As I got older I thought it was part of his life he would want to share with me. But he never got the chance. I'm sorry now I didn't ask him, maybe he never found the right time, or maybe I didn't give him one."

"You think I should ask her?"

"Yes, I do. She may have her reasons, but I think if she did confide in you she would feel an awful lot better."

"You're probably right. I know I have family up there who I've never met, and as far as I can tell they don't even know I exist." James suddenly felt very sad, wondering how his mother could lock him out. There was so much he didn't know or understand. And until this moment he had never realised the significance of it all.

"There has to be a reason David. There has to be."

"Your Mother would never knowingly hurt you. If she's hiding something then it has to be that she thinks she's protecting you."

"I know, but I still don't understand why or what reason there could possibly be to keep me away from Scotland. Sometimes I feel like an outsider, as though I don't really belong up there, even though my father was born and spent most of his life there.

"Maybe that time is drawing near. You said yourself she sounded distressed and not her usual self. Whatever it is up there, it brings her no joy and maybe if she could tell you, you could take away some of the pain."

"I think you're right David. Let's hope so, because I think the time has come."

"Do you want me to make myself scarce? "

"No I don't think so, whatever it is, I want you there. I feel as though you are somehow connected."

"Glad you said that, because that's how I feel. Strange isn't it, but I would never have been so presumptuous as to say it."

As they heard the car draw up they went out to greet her. Both James and David were shocked at her appearance.

"Hello," she whispered wanly. She was quiet and subdued with dark shadows that circled tired empty eyes. Her whole being had somehow lost that little bit of life that had put her apart from others. Never had they seen such a change in anyone in so short a space of time. His mother had always been so strong. Helping her upstairs, James suggested she take a nap before dinner and that they would speak her later. Maria smiled sadly, was grateful for their understanding and nodded in appreciation.

"I do feel a little tired." She said

"You look all in," he said tenderly/ "We've missed you. After you've had a rest you'll soon feel better."

"Could I just have a light snack in my room James?" She said trying to smile, but failing miserably.

"Of course mother, I'll organise it right away, just rest."

As they watched her slowly climb the stairs, her shoulders hunched and head down, they each felt in their own way so much love for this woman, and it pained them to see her like this.

"I wonder what has happened." David said.

"I don't know, but I feel as though I should go to her even if she doesn't want me. I feel as though in some way I can ease her pain."

Taking the stairs two at a time he reached his mother's room and pulling her tenderly into his arms he held her close. Her sadness hung heavy in the air as her glazed eyes refused to focus.

"Tomorrow we will talk, tonight rest," he said gently. Looking into her sad eyes he said, "Everything will be alright, I promise. Remember the brick wall."

And just at that moment Maria saw his father in him. And yes, the time had come for her to tell all to her son.

"You are so like your father, I loved him very much. You do know that don't you?"

"Yes mother I do. Now promise me you'll try to rest. Things will seem different in the morning just wait and see.

Maria sighed heavily, she knew it wouldn't. How do you tell your son his father was a homosexual and was shunned by everyone, including his great grandfather, and that was why, they never met. Or that his mother was classed as possessed and evil and had been told repeatedly that she was never wanted and didn't belong. And now, on top of all that, she was being blamed for her mother's breakdown. What more could she say. The tears fell silently down her face as she buried her head in the pillows, willing the world to go away.

Chapter Thirty Two.

James thought long and hard. He knew his mother was experiencing a period of extreme stress and didn't know why. He decided the problem must have something to do with her visit to Scotland, so the answer had to be back there, it had to be with her family. He knew there was a lot of bad feeling with them, a lot of history so bad she couldn't talk about it. But now he knew the time had come when his mother needed him. And if he was going to help her, he had to understand, he had to know what had gone on and why she was hurting so much. Just thinking about it angered him. His mother was a wonderful woman who wouldn't hurt anyone. Who did this so-called family of hers think they were that they could do this to her. He wasn't going to stand for it any longer. It had to be sorted once and for all, and if that meant he had to go up there himself, then that is what he would do.

The following day Maria realised it was time to tell the truth. She could tell by James's expression that the time had come. It was going to hurt, she knew that, but he had the right to know the truth, the whole truth. She could no longer protect him from the harsh realities of his grandparents. James insisted David should be present as he was practically one of the family, and Maria was glad because she didn't want any more secrets. David's father had been part of her life and she realised he had a right to know that.

The two of them sat there in stunned silence. James had realised years ago that his mother had had a turbulent childhood, but listening to her now, he realised just how bad it had been.

"The nice things that have happened to me during my life were with your father, James, and also with yours, David. Both in their own way brought me happiness." She paused to look at them both, hoping that they would realise just how good and kind their fathers were.

"Thank you," David said, "for being so honest. You have given me the opportunity to understand my father. He used to refer to a Maria often. Sometimes I used to wonder about his relationship with my mother even though I didn't know her as she died when I was born. Now I know the truth about you and my father I am happy. You've put my mind at rest. Underneath I knew my father was a good honest decent person, but he did have a faraway look in his eyes when he spoke of you."

"He was a wonderful man and would never have done anything that wasn't right." Maria said.

"Yes, I know. Thank you."

"But your father was the love of my life," she said turning to James. "There is one thing I just don't know how to put in words." She hesitated. "How do you say your father was a homosexual" she thought.

"If you're trying to tell me my father was a homosexual I know, I realised that years ago."

"You did? How? I mean... Oh I don't know what I mean. He did love us I know that, I believe it with my whole heart"

"I know. Remember, you saved all his letters and gave

them to me when I was old enough to read."

"Yes," she smiled.

"I know he loved us, but he did live with a partner and die with a terrible illness which today is called A.I.Ds" James said softly "but sadly it wasn't diagnosed then."

"I never thought about that." Maria said.

"You are so naive sometimes mother" he smiled. "In the fifties and sixties it wasn't accepted, but today in the eighties no one is shocked, people just get on with their own lives. I don't blame my great grandfather, it was the era he lived in, but he sounds like he was a pretty decent person."

"Yes, but I still wish you could have known him."

"After listening to what your family are like I wish you could have known him too," he said noticing the sadness, and the guilt which were still there in her eyes for all to see.

"Don't let your father destroy you mother. He's the one who is in the wrong. He's the one who is shifting the blame to make himself feel better." James said, taking her hand gently into his own.

"Why don't we all go up to Inverness. You can take me to the cottage in the hills where you said you feel close to dad. You always said he helped you and gave you strength, even in death you said he was there for you."

"Then let's go, the three of us. Besides, I do have some normal relatives I'd like you to meet – an auntie, two uncles and some cousins. Come on, let them see the real Maria."

"I think it's a wonderful idea, and also the right thing to so. Go to the cabin, regain your spirit and put your ghosts to rest. Together you will find the strength," David said. "I will keep everything going here and wait for you."

"Why, aren't you coming with us?" James said, looking at David.

"No. Because this is part of your life and you both need to address it personally."

James looked from David to his mother. She appeared to be so sad, so broken. He realised David was right. It was up to him. If he couldn't help his mother, no-one could. For the first time in his life he was filled with an uncontrollable rage which he wanted to unleash against those who had made his mother feel like this.

One phone call later to Cathy, and James had introduced himself, informed her that they were on their way up to the cottage and would be calling in to see her. He thought she sounded genuinely happy on the phone and said she couldn't wait to meet him.

It was a good journey, the weather was quite mild for September and his mother had slept most of the way. Against her wishes, James had decided to take the Rolls complete with Robert the chauffeur. He wasn't embarrassed about wealth as his mother was. Neither was he boastful. He just didn't see why they couldn't enjoy the comfort. His mother had, after all, worked hard all her life and at this moment in time she needed comforting. And he was going to make damned sure that's exactly what she was going to get. He wasn't interested in what the Scottish relatives thought.

Scotland was wonderful; James had never seen anything like it. The scenery was breath-taking, the rugged snow peaked mountains, the wild colours of the heathers and trees, made him understand his mother's love for the place. But he still couldn't understand why had she never spoken about it? Or if she loved it so much, why had she never gone back and taken him to show him that part of her life.

James knew there had been a reason. His mother had tried to explain it. But it was hard to understand how, after all these years, those people still had a hold over her. How come they were still capable of bringing so much pain and distress, "What hold could they possibly have on her?" he asked himself. He would soon find out, he would make it his business to put an end to it no matter what it took. Meanwhile he couldn't wait to see the cottage. His imagination was running wild. Would he be able to sense or even feel his father's presence? According to his mother, his father was unlike anyone else - talented, philosophical, sensitive and brilliant. He did think maybe she was exaggerating a little, but still he couldn't wait to get there and see this magical place where his father and grandparents had lived.

James was pleasantly surprised by the warm welcome he received from Cathy and her husband Gordon.

John arrived a little later, just in time for dinner, during which both John and Cathy expressed their concern over Maria's mental state. She was uncharacteristically quiet and withdrawn.

"Maybe after we've spent some time up in the cottage she will feel better." James said hopefully, glancing from John to Cathy.

"This is not like our Maria" John added. "He has a lot to answer for, him up there."

"We'll take you up to the cottage tomorrow after a good night's rest, and help you get comfortable." Cathy said.

James smiled, he really wanted to go up there and then but had to accept it was dark and he had no idea where it was. Plus, he wanted his mother to rest. She looked terribly exhausted.

Thanking them, he took his mother upstairs and after she was settled he also went to bed, thinking that tomorrow would be soon enough to ask questions.

They awoke the next morning to the smell of a good traditional cooked breakfast. James was ravenous and even his mother seemed to have found an appetite. Unfortunately breakfast was interrupted by a loud knock on the door. Pushing his plate away Gordon rose from the table to find a man hand holding three letters. They were, he informed Gordon, to be hand delivered only. Placing one in each of their hands, he then requested that they were all to sign in acknowledgement of receiving them. Maria first then John and lastly Cathy, he seemed very happy that Maria was there.

"Who's going to open it first," John smiled.

"I wonder who it's from?"

James and Gordon laughed.

"I think you might have to open them to find out."

"Okay" John said, "You are the oldest Maria, so come on, you first."

"Together," she said smiling, unable to muster up much enthusiasm.

The letter was from the solicitors in Inverness, requesting their presence in the house at 11 o'clock the following day for the reading of the will of James Fleming Snr. The house was apparently called 'Whispers' and Maria brightened as she thought of her James. He always called his home 'little whispers'. Surely it was too much of a coincidence. That crotchety old thing her grandfather, surely couldn't have picked a nice name like that. At first she wasn't going to bother going but now, well something inside her wanted her to go.

"Tomorrow, there is something I want you all to do for me."

"What would that be mother?" James said sensing the change in her manner.

"When we arrive I don't want you to say anything, even if you hear them being abusive to me."

"Why?"

"Because I have a feeling we will have the last laugh."

"You and your feelings, okay I promise."

"James, you don't know how nasty they are to your mother, I don't think you could stand there and say nothing."

"You may be right on that one Cathy," John said.

"Look I'm coming, I wouldn't miss it for the world. I know my mother's feelings and if she says she's going to have the last laugh, then that's what she'll have."

"Alright, but you have to promise, total silence."

"Deal."

Chapter Thirty Three.

The heart attack suffered by their father was not serious but the fall he had while still holding the knife was. This was the news given to John and Cathy after the accident, both of whom felt no emotion whatsoever towards him anymore. The blade had pierced his body at such an angle that it had done irretrievable damage to his spine.

"A million-to–one chance," the doctors said. "Unfortunately he will never walk again."

"Justice that's what I call it." John said almost smiling.

Anton went from being quiet, moody and deeply depressed to screaming, losing his temper and throwing anything that got in his way. No one could predict what mood he was going to wake up with. The feeling in the house was at its lowest. A heavy depression hung in the air as the staff tried to carry on as if nothing had happened. Then the death of Mr. James Fleming Snr. seemed to add to the depression.

It was the reading of the will and the atmosphere in the room was electrifying. Maria's grandparents looked at her in disgust, her grandfather tried to get her to leave stating she had no business there. He insisted that Maria was not part of the family and was not welcome, especially since she had caused the accident that had crippled Anton. The solicitor pointed out that the late Mr Fleming had requested she be there.

"Yes, but he's not family, I have never seen him before."

The grandfather said pointing to James.

Maria nodded discreetly to him and he left the room. She wanted to keep James's identity secret for the moment. James didn't understand why, but he quietly left the room, even though it was the last thing he wanted to do.

Maria looked at her mother and as usual she just smiled back, except now it broke Maria's heart to see her like that. "At least she doesn't understand anything, or what is happening" Maria thought, consoling herself.

Anton scowled in his wheelchair, he had become very bitter. Just as he thought the time had come when he was going to be very rich through his wife's money, he could no longer go out and enjoy it. How he hated his eldest daughter, "Evil bitch" he muttered under his breath.

Maria, John and Cathy didn't know why they were there, a great uncle who they had never met, wouldn't have left them anything. Although Maria had met him, he hadn't known who her parents were or who she was related to, even so they had met after he had made out his will.

"Could I have your attention please?" Mr Jackson the solicitor said in a clear voice.

A quiet hush descended in the room as her grandparents patiently waited for him to speak.

"To my brother Robert and his wife Fiona I leave an annual allowance of five thousand pounds each. To their daughter Ailsa, my niece, I leave five thousand pounds, to her

201

three children Maria, John and Cathy five thousand pounds."

"Wow" John exclaimed.

Cathy remained in shock.

"Come on get on with it" her grandfather rudely interrupted.

Ignoring the outburst and his bad manners, Mr Jackson continued in a slow and precise voice. He was not going to be hurried.

"To my grandson James, I leave my estate and all further monies.

"He can't do" grandfather said in shock, "what about this house, the land, they are mine. He promised."

All eyes turned to face him as the realisation came that, after all these years of him lording it about, he didn't actually own the property.

"Unfortunately," Mr Jackson said, "his grandson died whilst living in America."

"Thank God" Anton said under his breath.

"So it must come back to me then." Grandfather said, the relief could be heard in his voice.

"Would you please let me continue?" Mr Jackson said adjusting his glasses as he looked once more at the papers before him.

"He was married."

"Married" grandfather exploded. "He couldn't be. He was one of them there queer people. There has to be mistake."

Maria was now smiling as she was coming to realise the implications of the will and what it meant. Her father was angry but her grandfather was positively furious.

"I'll contest it," he said "it can't be right."

"Apparently, and it hasn't been confirmed yet, there is also a child involved." Mr Jackson seemed to be almost enjoying watching them squirm.

"And what are you smiling at you stupid bitch?" Anton shouted, seeing Maria's face.

"Don't you know what this means? We could all be homeless, and you're standing there smiling like an idiot.

"You may all continue to reside here until the true owner has been located, at this moment in time we are not sure if she is in America or Scotland.

"You mean she could be a yank?"

"If you mean could she be an American Mr Fleming, I can only say that until we meet she could be any nationality."

"What if she is in America? Where will that leave us?"

"It will leave you exactly as you are now. Waiting to see what she decides to do with the estate."

"Oh God," Anton sighed, "we could all be homeless. And then, as he fully realised what has happened, he turned and screamed at Maria. "It's your fault. You've only ever brought us bad luck. Now look at us, we are broke and probably homeless. How am I expected to look after your mother?"

Maria didn't even justify it with an answer, though she couldn't help smiling a little. Their faces were a picture, her grandfather was red with fury, grandmother white with shock and her father alternated from one to the other. At one stage she thought he was going to pass out he had gone so white. John and Cathy wore a wide happy smile. Only her mother seemed to be out of place, she looked frightened and confused.

"Thank you Mr Jackson," Maria said standing, holding out her hand, "I will call on you tomorrow to give you my home address." And smiling she turned, "Goodbye for now my dear family, I'm sure we will meet again."

Maria couldn't help it. She laughed out loud at the look on their faces, especially her father's. He was livid at the audacity of her laughing at their bad luck.

The door closed after her and the room fell into a deathly

silence, only Maria's soft laughter could be heard. It was as if she was mocking them.

A distinct chill could be felt. For all their shouting and outward confidence each one of them felt some kind of fear.

Chapter Thirty Four.

"It is time" she said "to tell you James, and Cathy and John, why I kept my marriage a secret."

As Maria spoke all words were heard in disbelief. No one had any idea of what had been happening. Cathy and John felt as though somewhere along the line they had really let Maria down. They hadn't really known about the fall out with her mother and grandparents. They had heard of it but had never taken it on board. Now though they realised they had been too full of their own lives to think of Maria, and that saddened them.

"You were married?" Cathy said "And we didn't know."

"Why didn't you say something?"

"I couldn't John. Take your mind back. We were just children. They would only have tried to annul it or something."

"I'm sorry for not telling you, but we made a pact. We promised never to tell anyone, it was our own little bit of happiness."

"I can understand that" John said reluctantly, still feeling a little hurt.

"And then I discovered I was pregnant," she said smiling at James.

"How could you keep him a secret all these years?"

"I know. I realise now what I should have done, but then it was different. Both of you lived up there with them and everyone hated James, thought he was a freak. I couldn't take the chance of them finding out." Maria turned to her son. "I was protecting your father. He was a wonderful person and I didn't want anyone to say anything different."

"It must have been hard for you Maria, how did you manage?" Cathy asked.

"I lived with Ada, well had my own room, and Tim and Laura upstairs. You do you remember them?" They both nodded.

"Well they helped me. Then I decided my son would never know what it was like to be hungry. He was going to have everything that money could buy, but more importantly he was going to be loved."

James smiled at his mother, as the tears welled up behind his eyes. At last he fully realised what her life had really been like.

"After that I spent most of my time making sure he would want for nothing. I built a large successful business thinking that was all I'd ever want for us both. I knew what it was like to be hungry and dirty with nowhere to live and so I had to make money. I had to be successful. And I had to do it myself. That's all I lived for. I wanted never to know poverty, again."

"And now Maria, what do you think now?" Cathy inquired.

"I have missed out, I put money and fear before my family and I'm sorry for that."

"I think we are all guilty of putting our own life first. You did what you thought was best for James. And I think you were right." John said thoughtfully. "But the past is past, and from now on we will always be together. I have my sister back and a nephew" he said smiling.

"I couldn't agree more." Cathy added. "But what are you going to do now?"

"I don't know, I need to think and also talk it over with James", she said turning to him.

"What about them up there? Are you going to tell them?" Cathy said, smiling at what she could only imagine would be their reaction.

"No, not yet, it's our secret" she smiled. "See, I can't go through life without secrets. I am feeling very weary, and a little lost. I don't know what to do about the inheritance. Everything that I thought would happen, never."

"You're thinking of what father said now aren't you? Well don't, it wasn't your fault and he is evil for saying it."

"I know."

"But you don't know, Maria we were just kids, and you

thought you were protecting ma.”

“Yes I suppose.” She answered.

But John and Cathy could tell by her voice she had taken it badly and was blaming herself. Their inheritance had paled into insignificance as they remembered their father's taunting accusation. Both John and Cathy would never forgive him. Maria didn't deserve it and they hated him for the pain he had inflicted on her. They were not going to forget it.

Chapter Thirty Five.

Natalie looked idly through the window, she was bored. At twenty eight she felt as though life was passing her by. Just when everything was there within her reach, it had all came tumbling down. Her mother had died suddenly. That was three years ago, and since then she had left university safely holding her degree but putting away all her dreams and ambitions.

"Good morning my dear, how are you today?"

"Fine thank you, father," she answered.

"You look more beautiful each day" he said, kissing her affectionately on the cheek. Natalie smiled, and smoothing down her fine golden hair she retouched her lipstick as the reflection in the mirror let her know that her pale complexion needed a little colour.

"I think you look absolutely wonderful the way you are."

Natalie swirled round to see who had entered the office without her knowing. She was surprised and quite shocked to find that someone could actually enter without her knowing. But as she returned his slightly arrogant smile she realised that, without question, he had to be one of the most handsome men she had encountered in a long time. Slowly she studied him: tall around 6ft.2in, quite well built with a defined physique you could only achieved in the gym, eyes that held confidence, warmth, and a bright sparkle that shone with a childish look. He reminded her of the life she once knew, a life she desperately wanted back but knew it would not at this moment in time be possible.

He ran his hand through the soft curls that hung almost untidily around his face. The movement interrupted her thoughts, bringing her back to reality, to her life as it was.

"Do I meet with your approval?" he said, sounding amused as he continued to watch her appraisal of him.

"I'm sorry, please forgive me, it's not something I would normally do, but...."

"Please," he interrupted "think nothing of it" then he smiled a wide infectious smile showing the most perfect set of white teeth. His tanned skin glowed with the golden tones only acquired on an exotic beach. "It certainly wasn't in the highlands of Scotland," she thought. "As beautiful as they were, it defiantly wasn't a paradise in the sun."

Natalie became aware of her own behaviour and felt totally lost for words.

"Shall we start again?" he said extending his hand. "My name is James Fleming and I would like to speak to Mr Jackson of Jackson and Jackson." He smiled. I take it, it is father and son."

"It could be father and daughter."

"Is it?"

"No actually, it was Mr Jackson deceased and his son. Now, though, there is a daughter."

"And you are?"

"Ms Jackson." She smiled. "Pleased to meet you."

Taking her hand in his he slowly looked into her eyes.

"You are far too young and attractive to be a staid old solicitor."

"Thanks for the back handed compliment, but we'll have less of the old. And yes I am a solicitor."

"Are you a happy one?"

"Maybe we should keep to the business at hand." she said briskly.

James Fleming became acutely aware he had hit a raw nerve and for that he was truly sorry. He wouldn't have offended her for anything. In fact, quite the opposite. For all his good looks he was quite shy when it came to the opposite sex and he realised he had tried too hard to impress her.

"Am I having my hand smacked," he said sheepishly.

She couldn't help but return his smile.

"What do you want Mr Fleming?"

"O.K. back to business, I would like Mr Jackson to come up and meet my mother. At the moment we are staying in a most delightful cottage up in the Glen. It's called 'The Whispers' on..."

"I know where it is Mr Fleming. In fact, your name is well known here in town."

"I don't think so," he said quite coldly. "This is my first visit to these parts."

Too late, Natalie realised it was she who had now overstepped the mark, and for this she was deeply upset. Because somewhere deep inside her he had stirred some long lost feelings. Feelings she neither wanted nor trusted anymore.

Taking the diary she offered him two dates when her father was available. Both of which he said were unacceptable.

"Can't you attend yourself?" he asked. "You are qualified aren't you?"

"Mr Fleming, I am a fully qualified lawyer." Her indignation was obvious. "And I do," she emphasised "specialise in criminal law."

Why she felt the need to justify herself she didn't know.

"Shall we say three o' clock tomorrow afternoon."

"I look forward to it already" and taking her hand in his, shook it in an almost tender way. Then he was gone.

Natalie went to the window. She couldn't help it, she wanted to see him, to see him walk. Part of it was her training. She was fascinated by criminal psychology and observed every one she could. She had to admit that he was a pleasure to watch.

Quite suddenly the most impressive car she had ever seen stopped just yards from the office door. A deep silver grey with the touch of a blue sheen gave this wonderful car a character all of its own. A Rolls Royce, something she had seen mainly in magazines. A smartly dressed chauffeur deftly left the driver's seat to open the door for his passenger. It was him. Her heart almost stopped. Not only was he gorgeous with a great sense of humour, he was rich.

On hearing who the new client was, Mr Jackson cancelled his appointment and accompanied his daughter the following day to meet Mrs Fleming.

"It must be the Mrs Fleming who has just inherited the estate." He felt so elated it shone in his face. "Oh I do hope so, it isn't very often we get interesting cases especially one involving those from up the glen."

"Yes I know" she answered quietly as she thought of all the mundane paper work that was piling up on her desk. She had promised her father five years of a working partnership but was finding it harder and harder as time slipped slowly by. Natalie knew her father was banking on the fact she would come to love living at home and hopefully find a nice young man to marry and live happily ever after.

If only he knew, she was counting the days when her time was up. When that promise she made after her mother's funeral was fulfilled. And then she was off. Once she would have settled down, once she thought she was in love. But then he shown his true colours and it was nothing like it was supposed to be. She vowed she would never trust another man again. To Natalie there was a life out there, a life she was desperately waiting to live.

"Natalie, what's to do with you? It's not like you not to concentrate." Her father interrupted. "What is he like does he have an American accent?"

"No he was English"

"Oh" her father sounded disappointed. "They could still be characters" he said hopefully. "From what I've heard about Mr J. Fleming Jnr. he was, to say the least, different."

"You mean he was a homosexual? I've read the file father, but how do we know if it's true?"

"We don't, and anyway it doesn't really matter. If this lady has a valid marriage certificate, then she was his legal wife. And by law, that's all that counts at this moment in time." Then a large grin spread across his face.

"What are you thinking now?"

"Only of the inhabitants of the big house, those who have looked down on everybody for as long as I can remember," he almost laughed out loud." Just think," he smiled, "they are about to become poor and homeless."

"She may let them stay."

"I don't think so my dear. It's a large estate and a lot of money is involved. I think she will either live in it or sell it." he said.

"Oh there was one thing father, did I tell you he came down in a Rolls Royce, complete with chauffeur."

Mr Jackson stopped in his tracks, "What did you say?"

"I think you heard." she laughed.

"This gets better by the minute" he smiled.

James couldn't wait for the appointed time. Natalie had invaded his thoughts. It had been a long time since anyone had affected him like this. He was besotted; she was tall and willowy yet had all the womanly shapes a man would die for. She appeared delicate, soft, and feminine. Yet had an edge that portrayed an underneath strength that warned you not to underestimate her. He loved the way she smiled, her head slightly leaning to the left as her lips parted. Full lips, soft and well defined, had always been his weakness, and as he dreamt of her he could feel his lips, brushing against hers. He could feel his passion rising and wanted, no needed, to pull her close and crush his lips against hers, run his hands gently over that beautiful body and feel the touch of her hair that hung like silken thread in warm shades of auburn as it fell around her shoulders, enveloping the most perfect delicate skin that reminded him of porcelain. James knew she was perfect for him. There had been that something special between them. He had felt it in an instant, and he knew she had too.

On arriving home later that day, his face was still positively glowing. He had never felt so alive, so attracted to anyone like this before.

"I see someone is happy" Maria said with a knowing smile.

"I've had a good day thank you mother" he smiled," I did try to get an appointment with Mr Jackson for tomorrow but unfortunately he was out of the office and is unable to come tomorrow."

"So why are you smiling?"

"Because the most wonderful vision of womanhood, who just happens to be his daughter, is fully qualified."

"Fully qualified?"

"I mean as a solicitor she's also a lawyer and she's coming here tomorrow."

"Well she has certainly made an impression on you. I can't wait to meet her."

Maria smiled, seeing her son look so happy lifted her depression. She realised then that was where her heart should be, in the future. Watching her son fall in love, getting married, having children and doing all the normal things in life. She thought of his father, "Live for now" is what he would have said. "You can't change people, you can't make them be as you would want them to be. But that doesn't mean you allow them to hurt you. Dismiss those that offend the spirit of life, always remember the brick wall, and live your life.'" Maria sighed, as she remembered what he used to say to her. "I wish you were here James, I feel so alone sometimes." She knew what she had to do but it was hard.

Maria realised there had been times when she had forgotten about her brick wall, and allowed her father to nearly destroy her. "Then I really would have lost," she realised as she looked at her sons happy countenance as he read through the files on the table. Impulsively she stood and walking over to him, kissed his head affectionately.

James looked at her enquiringly, his mother wasn't given to displays of affection.

"Don't worry, I've not lost it," she said, "In fact I have just found it, we are going to be alright, I promise. I'm not going to be vindictive, there has been enough sadness. I just need to make sure my mother, your grandmother is happy in whatever world she lives in."

James stood up and hugged his mother.

"I'm so glad you have come back to me."

"Was I that bad?"

"I was worried for a time there, but tell me, what brought about the change?"

"You looking happy, the look you only get when you've met someone special. And something your father taught me, which I had momentarily forgotten."

"Well whatever, I can relax now and leave your inheritance in your very capable hands."

"And the girl?" she enquired.

"She doesn't even know yet. Give me a chance, we only met yesterday and that was for only a few minutes."

"Sounds like love at first sight to me."

"I refuse to justify that one with an answer."

Maria laughed, "You don't have to" and for the first time in weeks she felt happy.

Chapter Thirty Six.

Slowly the car moved along the winding road towards the cottage. Each bend seemed more dangerous than the last.

"I take it you don't drive too often up these roads," Natalie laughed.

"No, and it's only because I'm curious who the wife is that I'm here. You are more than capable. But you have to admit, it is going to be quite amusing seeing that family squirm. It' the best thing that's happened this year. I can't wait to see the outcome." Natalie smiled as she realised even her father got bored.

James was surprised to see both Mr Jackson and his daughter. She still looked wonderful he thought to himself as he gazed at her very smart business suit. Perfectly tailored hiding those lovely curves and her hair was now tied back in a very austere kind of knot at the back of her head. He smiled as he realised she had done this on purpose.

This time it was Natalie who was being admired and she smiled to herself as she remembered yesterday. Today, though, she knew he was rich and that made a huge difference to how she felt. She had come to the conclusion he could probably have whoever he wanted and decided it definitely wasn't going to be her. She was not interested.

Introductions were made and Mr Jackson stared hard at Maria. He felt as though they had met before but couldn't place it. She was strikingly attractive, perfectly groomed with a very easy manner. How could he forget such a woman?

"Yes" she said, looking at him. "We have met it was at the reading of the will of the late Mr Fleming Snr."

Then the realisation hit him, she was that Maria. The Maria they were all hostile towards.

"I don't understand?" he said.

"Well no-one actually knows who I am. To the family I am Maria, the one to blame for all injustices. They don't know I am the widow of the late James Jnr. Or the fact he has a son.

"Forgive me if I'm talking out of turn, but you looked, how can I say, quite poor when we last met."

"Yes Mr Jackson, I may be a business woman and independently wealthy, but at this moment in time I see no reason to display any sign of wealth."

He smiled knowingly.

"Have you made any kind of plans regarding the estate?"

"No, until I have decided what to do, they can stay in ignorance. Both my brother John and Cathy know of my inheritance but I prefer no one else to know, that's not a problem is it?"

"Absolutely not" he said.

"The only change at the moment is with my brother John. Make him the official manager of the estate including the house. Also secure a budget for any investments he deems necessary or if he needs any extra staff. Finally, give him a healthy wage. When I do make a decision on the rest of my dear family I will be in touch. Meanwhile, I would appreciate your descretion."

"Whatever you wish," Mr Jackson said smiling. He was enjoying every minute of this.

"Thank you. Meanwhile if Ms Jackson....

"Please call me Natalie."

"Well Natalie, if you could return my papers for me I would be most appreciative. I don't always trust the post with important documents."

"That will be no problem."

"Thank you. I think we will be working together quite often over the next few months, so please feel free to drop the formalities, It's Maria."

Natalie smiled, she felt relaxed. Maria was a person whom she could admire, straight talking and no frills, precise and knowing exactly what she wanted. But, more importantly, she came across as a very honest and forthright person who would not accept anything less than what she wanted.

"Business over" James said, "It's time for refreshments."

A young girl who his mother had employed to look after them promptly arrived with a tray laden with cakes and sandwiches. Looking at Natalie, James smiled. He knew he hadn't given her a chance to leave early. This was also noted by her, and, determined she wasn't going to play his little game, she studiously ignored him.

Her father noticed and wasn't too happy.

"There's a delightful story attached to the 'Little Whisper' he said trying to regain some sort of intimacy.

"The Little Whisper?" both Maria and James enquired together.

Having their attention Mr Jackson continued happily. He needed their business, but more importantly, he was finding it all very interesting. Why his daughter was behaving the way she was, was beyond him. She was normally very efficient and charming. He would have to have a word with her later.

"My father went school with your grandparents, they were close friends. He told me that, whenever they had the chance, your grandparents would spend as much time up here as they could. In those days it wasn't deemed proper to be alone with someone of the opposite sex and you couldn't spend time alone together, so they often invited friends to join them. My father said they were so in love they just used to sit holding hands and whispering sweet words of love to each other."

"How romantic" Maria said.

"It became a saying, and then the cottage progressed to

becoming known as 'the Little Whispers.' They adored each other and after they were married insisted on living there, they wanted to make it their home. An extension was built when they discovered your grandmother was going to have a baby. That was your father" he said smiling at James.

James thought it was wonderful listening to someone who knew his family.

"Meanwhile, unknown to them, your great grandfather bought the estate and spent a small fortune turning it into a magnificent home. He knew how much your grandfather loved the land and had an affinity with it. He was always at his best when working with nature."

"Just like John" Maria commented.

"Yes and he named what has become known as the big house, 'The Whispers'. Everyone was so happy." Mr Jackson paused as a wave of sadness washed over him. "Then tragedy struck," he said.

"There was an accident, both your grandparents died. They never had the chance to move into the house. Your father was brought up by his grandfather, but he could never bring himself to live in the house or sell it. To him, 'Little Whispers' as the cottage had become affectionately known, was the place he loved most. That was where his son loved to be, and where his grandson had been born."

"What happened then regarding the big house?" James asked.

"He let his younger brother live in it until such time as your father was old enough to know what he wanted in life."

"Then what happened?"

"Well apparently James said he didn't want to live in the house and had no desire to work the land. It was then, when his grandfather asked him about his future and suggested he might have sons who would want to work the land, that James admitted he was homosexual."

"I can see how that would have gone down," James said. "He must have been very strong to admit to that in those days."

"Yes" Mr Jackson continued, "Unfortunately there was a row which was followed by James being ostracised from the family. The cottage was his, as was a small inheritance left by his parents. He refused to ask or accept anything from his grandfather. They never spoke again."

"How sad" Maria murmured.

"Years later, James wrote out of the blue and said he was married and had a son. His grandfather was overjoyed at hearing from him and wanted to meet. He sent letter after letter but heard nothing until one day a brief note came informing him of James's death. I don't think he ever got over it; he blamed himself for being weak and not supporting him. He really did love him you know."

"What a sad story" James said, "I can almost feel his grief"

"Yes it is sad isn't it. He made his will out and then lived for the day I could find James's wife. He thought she must be American, because James lived and died there. He wanted so much to meet you Maria, but unfortunately it wasn't to be," he said sadly.

"You know," she said almost in a whisper "for some reason I felt as though I had to find him. To tell him James had been very happy and that he loved him dearly. And that he knew how hard it must have been for him to understand."

"You must have second sight, but sadly he died......

"Yes" she said, interrupting him quietly, "he died holding my hand."

Chapter Thirty Seven.

It was a tranquil day, Maria felt at peace. James was still pursuing Natalie who Maria had to admit was good for him. There was no doubt in Maria's mind that they loved each other. Why young people behaved the way they did never ceased to amaze her. Still as long as they were happy, wasn't that the important thing.

Since the reading of the will John had really come into his own. He had five thousand pounds, an excellent job that he enjoyed immensely and good wages. Now his thoughts were governed by planning his own wedding in the early spring. Although his confidence had grown since he had become estate manager, it was his inner confidence that had become apparent. He now lived in a house in which he had overall control, not his parents' or grandparents; house, but his. And they had to respect him.

It had been John's job to inform his grandparents that they were to move into one of the cottages on the estate and that they could live there rent free as long as they helped to look after his mother. Maria had decided that a little humility would do them good.

Ailsa was looking good. Her eyes no longer had the deep dark circles that used to surround them. The unhealthy pallor of her skin was now gone and she had once again recaptured the smooth youthful glow she was once so proud of. And her hair was definitely her crowning glory.

From a distance she appeared healthy and happy. But on closer inspection the same empty eyes stared back at you.

"If only your mind could be cleared Ma, I know somewhere inside you, you are still there." Maria said tenderly as she looked at her.

The ownership of the estate was still a mystery to her grandparents and parents. Only Cathy and John knew of Maria's marriage and what the true lineage of James was.

Because Ailsa was still childlike and couldn't cope with change, she had freedom of the house and also, as much as it pained Maria, her father was allowed to stay there also, although it was on the strict understanding that he was only welcome as long as Ailsa wanted and needed him.

Maria was spending more and more time at the cottage, going only to Manchester when business absolutely demanded it. David was more than capable of running the business. He had matured into a lovely young man and had found himself falling in love with a very pretty young Jewish girl he had met at one of his family occasions. He had always maintained he would marry only for love, but Maria was pleased that he had fallen in love with someone so like himself. Apart from sharing the same beliefs, she was also ambitious, headstrong and had a very good business mind on her.

Maria could see three weddings on the horizon – James's, David's and John's - and couldn't wait. She was getting the family she had always wanted and hoped lots of children would follow. She no longer had any desire to have a relationship with anyone. Her life was at last starting to settle. She accepted the fact she would always have that little niggling feeling at the back of her mind about not belonging. But it was the way she was brought up, it was circumstanced. There was nothing she could do about it. Her priorities now, were building a strong family unit. Over the years she had made enough money to last them all a life time but realised it was love that was the most precious thing. And she was looking forward to spending the rest of her life enjoying it.

Over the past few months Maria's appearance had changed a lot. Gone was the neat stylish auburn hair, instead she had allowed her own natural colour to come through. It was still thick and dark but had just a sprinkling of grey which added to her beauty, hanging once more onto her shoulders in deep waves. No longer did she wear the smart tailored suits or the high heeled shoes which gave her legs an elegant line.

You could now see her out walking in casual trousers and loose tops in pretty colours, or sometimes she would wear very vibrant colours as if she was showing the world she was at last herself. Her hair was mostly tied back loosely and her face free of cosmetics. Maria felt free and it was a feeling she never wanted to lose.

"When are you going to tell them Maria?"

"I haven't decided John, it doesn't feel right at the moment. I don't know why, but it just isn't the right time."

"Well I am not going to argue with your feelings, they kept us alive years ago." John said smiling, "but I have to tell you, mother is inviting her parents up more and more. "

"That's up to you. If you are happy with it that's fine by me. The house is yours John to run as you see fit. As long as Ma is happy, I'm happy."

"The only problem I have Maria, is with Da,"

"Why what's he doing now?"

"He is becoming more aggressive and bad tempered with each new day. I don't know whether he is in pain or it's just him being him."

"I don't care about him, he is there only as long as Ma is happy, and wants him there."

"Yes, I know Maria, I was just saying, you know, keeping you informed. It is your estate after all and I know you want what is best for Ma. I have noticed a slight difference in her lately, especially when she has been down visiting our Cathy and playing with the bairns."

"How do you mean, what kind of difference?"

"It's hard to explain, but something's happening I'm sure, inside her head."

"If only that could be true," Maria sighed

"Why don't you come up Maria. She would like you to visit more I'm sure of it."

Maria became quiet. she loved her mother and did want to spend more time with her, but it was him. How could she pretend to be happy with her mother when she knew her father would be there?

"I'm sorry John, and I don't understand it myself, but there is a part of me that is still afraid. Forty years old," she smiled, "and still feared of the past."

"What is it you used to say about the brick wall?" John interrupted quietly.

"Yes, but how can I confront something I know nothing of? How can I put my fears away if I don't know what they are."

John's heart went out to his sister. She was still emotionally wrecked for all the outward signs of contentment and peace. He wished there was something he could do.

"Maybe there is" he thought.

Chapter Thirty Eight.

Ailsa and her mother stood looking out of the window, each in their own world. Ailsa saw the blue sky, her eyes focusing on the enormous expanse of space, trying to understand what was around her. She smiled, and turning to her mother asked if it was all real.

"You shouldn't be thinking or worrying, about what is real and what isn't, we love you as you are. Don't we Anton?" she said without looking at Ailsa.

Ailsa looked from one to the other, thinking her mind was playing games with her. Shadows and memories she didn't understand kept invading her thoughts. She didn't know what they were, except that she was frightened. They were horrible scenes that would not go away. Each day brought new memories and she had no one to talk to, no one to ask. She had tried, but her mother wouldn't listen and her husband, who was involved in most of these horrible memories, just got angry and called her stupid. Ailsa felt as though she was living in a kind of dream world, not knowing what was real and what wasn't. But inside her there was the feeling that something was missing, something was wrong. She didn't know what, or how she was involved, or even if she was involved, but her head hurt when she thought about it and she needed to know.

"I want Maria to come and see me." she declared one morning.

"Well she isn't coming. She's not wanted here." Anton said angrily. "I never want to see her again. Have you forgotten it was her who put me in this wheelchair? She took away my life, never forget that. Your daughter is nothing but a witch. She's evil."

"She is your daughter as well"

"No she isn't, and I don't want to talk about her ever again, do you understand" he bellowed, his face turning red with anger.

"Why are you behaving like this?" Ailsa's mother interrupted. "You know how Anton feels about her. You should be grateful he's here beside you. Many another man wouldn't have put up with the kind of illness you have. They would have put you away."

"That's true, you are a mental case and I don't need all this aggravation."

"Put me away?" Ailsa repeated. Something in the back of her mind came into place. Suddenly she wanted to see Maria.

"I want to see my daughter, if you don't send for her then I will go to her, I want Maria."

Within seconds Anton had moved across to where she was sitting, his wheelchair pressing up against her legs.

"You're hurting me Anton."

Grabbing her arm he stared into her eyes.

"Don't you remember what real pain is." he said menacingly. "You and that bitch of a daughter. I should have killed her when I had the chance. But don't you worry your stupid little head because, I promise you, one day I will." If he hadn't been so caught up in his anger he would have noticed Ailsa's face had changed. There was a spark of reality in her eyes as she stared into the face of the man who called himself her husband. The memories started to fall in place.

And then he cried out. It was a loud frightened cry, he clutched his chest. His eyes wide open in disbelief as he looked down and saw the blood pumping from him.

Ailsa's hand fell from the knife, she saw the blood and smiled.

"Now I remember, I remember your knife Anton. Are you hurting? I remember when I was hurting. I remember when Maria was hurting. You are not going to hurt us again, are you Anton?"

Chapter Thirty Nine.

The road seemed longer and narrower than Maria remembered as she drove at a snail's pace. She couldn't go any faster as the rain pelted down hitting the windows with a loud swish as the windscreen wipers worked furiously trying to clear the way. It was no use, she had to slow down. It was too dangerous.

"Please Maria, please you have to come" The voice was high pitched and out of control. The terror and the urgency of the call filled her with a sense of foreboding.

"What has happened?" she had asked, her heart pounding waiting for the answer, but the phone went dead. Alice was obviously in shock "but why?" Maria's insides screamed with the fear of what might have happened. Before getting into the car she had telephoned John, hoping he would be able to get there soon. Frustration mounted at her inability to go any faster. Every nerve in her body was stretched. She knew something terrible had happened, but what?

"Please God, don't let it be Ma. Please" and once again Maria felt the hopelessness of childhood when she was unable to help the mother she so desperately needed.

"John, meet me at the house." He could hear the urgency in Maria's voice, feel her fear. "And John, come alone." And then the phone went dead. He couldn't think what could possibly have happened, but he was already putting on his coat, picking up his keys and kissing goodbye to Morag his fiancée.

Maria and John both arrived at the same time. The house was eerily silent. Together they searched the rooms until they found the Library, Maria gasped, and John just stood open mouthed. Both found it hard to take in the scene. Their mother was sitting with eyes glazed covered in blood. It was as if she was out of this world, and trying to make sense of another. And then she started crying, heart rendering cries that came from the very depth of her soul. With these cries came the word "Maria, Maria," over and over again she repeated her daughter's name.

Anton lay gasping as Ailsa's mother looked on in shock. He was unable to move, apart from the slight movement of his hand as it held the knife which was still lodged in his chest. At first Maria thought he was dead. Ailsa fell to the floor her eyes transfixed on Anton. She had gone into shock. There was blood everywhere.

"Oh God Maria, what are we to do?" Alice cried, realising she should have phoned for an ambulance, but her hatred of Anton stopped her doing anything that might prevent his death. She had always loved Ailsa and could never forgive him or his wife for what they had done to her.

On hearing Maria's name, Ailsa came to life. She started crying softly and held out her arms to her.

John continued to stare. It was bizarre. His father lay dying, his mother seemed to have regained her memory except she thought it was forty years ago. And Maria had tears in her eyes.

Overwhelmed by the sheer strength of her mother's emotion as she wrapped her arms around her, Maria could only just make out what had happened. Her mother continued

to whisper how much she loved her, and though she was glad
her mother had recognised her, it didn't alter the fact she had
to know what had happened.

Ailsa wouldn't let go of Maria. Her arms were locked as she
moved back and forth holding Maria tight as you would a
child, whispering sweet words of comfort. Telling her not to
worry, saying he couldn't hurt her now, she would look after
her. And as Maria felt the strength of her arms around her,
felt the warm kisses on her cheek and heard her mother
whispering. "Mama loves you, Mama loves you" Maria
couldn't help but feel a little sense of happiness. Her life
seemed to be coming together and yet her father was there on
the floor bleeding to death, or maybe already dead. The scene
was unreal. She gently prised her mother's arms away, she had
to think, and quick.

"Take my mother down to your cottage," she said turning
to her grandmother who was now quiet but stared as if she
was frozen to the spot.

"Alice, who else knows what's gone on?"

"No one I swear, I kept them in here till you came. We
haven't spoken to anyone."

"Have you phoned anyone else, an ambulance or the
police?"

"No" she said guiltily

"Good," Maria said, Alice was instantly relieved.

"I think we should call them Maria," John interrupted.

"Yes, you do that John." Turning to Alice she said very carefully, "now tell me exactly what happened.

"It had something to do with a knife. Your Ma was her usual self one minute and then suddenly there was screaming and shouting and your Ma and Pa they were really arguing. At first I just stood there because I thought it was good that your Ma had recovered. But then he, your Pa, went over and whatever he said it made your Ma real mad. Something about 'you will never hurt her again'. Then he was taunting her about some fire. Your grandmother then told me to leave. I think she was embarrassed. She was telling them to behave properly."

"Then what?"

"Well I hadn't gone very far before I heard her screaming, so I went back in again. It was just as you saw, except your Ma was sitting next to him with blood all over her and he" she said indicating Anton "had a knife stuck in his chest."

Maria almost smiled. The way Alice spoke you would never believe she was talking about someone who was bleeding to death in front of her.

"Then your Ma stated to cry like a child. I think she'd retreated back into her own world again," she said. "At least I hope so" she added. And then she suddenly realised the significance of all that had happened.

"What are we to do?" she cried "They'll put her away."

Then turning to Maria she cried "They can't do that. It wasn't her fault. She would never survive. What's going to happen?"

"I don't want you to repeat any of what has happened tonight. Do you understand."

Alice looked at Maria waiting for an explanation; she knew the police were bound to question her.

Maria's mind was working fast. The fire! At last she knew there was something real in her fear of the fire in her nightmares. It did have something to do with him and it had caused her mother to come out of her twilight world to kill him.

She couldn't help it, inside she felt as though a great weight had lifted, and with it came a weird kind of peace. "It had been for her." That small sentence was what she had waited a lifetime to hear.

"Alice, this is what we're going to say happened. You were not in the house tonight. You were down at the cottage with Ma, visiting her parents. Do you understand?"

Alice nodded as she realised the true significance of what Maria was saying.

Turning to her grandmother she took her by the shoulders and spoke quietly but forcefully. "Stop crying" she said "and pull yourself together. You were not here tonight. You were at home with Ma."

Her grandmother looked at her as if she had never seen her before.

"Do you understand?"

Still she didn't answer. Maria again took her by the shoulders and this time, shook her vigorously. It had the desired effect.

"Yes, yes we weren't here." she said.

"Tonight, in this room, none of you saw anything. None of you were here"

She looked around, saw her father was now obviously dead and placed a blanket over him. Ailsa was still in a trance, which Maria was glad about. It was one of those rare moments when she realised her mother's illness was a blessing that would protect her from the pain of reality. Her grandmother still seemed shocked and dazed, but was beginning to get herself together, Alice she knew would do anything for her Ma. That just left John.

"Right go! Take Ma to the cottage, and remember" Maria said to her grandmother "you weren't here, and haven't been all night. If you utter one word to anyone, I will say you killed him. Do you understand?

"Yes" she nodded, knowing that Maria probably would do that.

"Now go, before the police arrive."

John who had remained quiet now looked at Maria in disbelief.

"I hope I am hearing things and you are not going to what I think you are."

"I can't let her get locked up John I can't. It will destroy her. It was the first time, the first time she did something just for me, and now I am doing something for her."

"And what about you, what will happen to your life?"

"I am young."

"No Maria, you can't do it, think! There's James to consider, it will break his heart."

"I know, but I have no choice, I have to do this. Please John, support me. It is something I have to do if I am ever to be rid of my ghosts. Do it for me, if not for Ma"

"I don't know Maria."

"Please John, promise me you want tell anyone."

Before he could answer the police arrived and took control of the situation. Maria gave a statement. She admitted killing her father. John full of anguish left the room.

Chapter Forty.

What he was hearing was wrong, he couldn't believe it. His brain refused to take it in. Why it was only four weeks ago his mother had seemed so happy saying she was going to up to `Little Whispers` to relax and spend some time with her own mother. So what could have gone so terribly wrong? As he packed his bags his mind couldn't rationalise anything. One minute he was waving off Natalie having spent the most wonderful weekend showing her all the sights in Manchester, his mother phoning him, overjoyed at the way the relationship was going, and now this.

It couldn't be true, and yet John had told him all that had happened so very clearly.

The phone rang. It was David returning his call.

"Thank God, David. It's my mother." He quickly told David all he knew, his heart was thumping and his breathing was laboured.

"James I'm coming over, we'll go up together."

"She didn't do it David, I know she didn't."

"I know that, try not to worry. I won't be long." True to his word he arrived just as James had finished packing.

"There has to be a reason, she wouldn't admit to killing him for nothing."

"The answer has to lie with her mother James."

"But that's just it, her mother wasn't there. That's what I don't understand. Why would she visit if she knew she wasn't there? And if she didn't know why did she stay? She hated her father. "

All the way up the two boys tried to figure out how it had happened, but nothing made sense. James was convinced that John knew more than he was letting on, and was feeling more agitated and frustrated by the minute.

It was late when they arrived. John was waiting for them but Cathy was at home with her children, apparently too distraught to speak. James couldn't see his mother and that made it worse. He was totally overcome with emotion. John offered no insight as to what or why it had happened making both James and David sceptical. They didn't believe him.

Natalie arrived and took them to the hotel she had booked them into. Both James and David felt as though they couldn't stay with John in the big house or with Cathy, and `Little Whispers` was too far out of town. They wanted to feel as though they were near to Maria.

"Something's wrong David"

"I agree, but what?"

"I just wish I didn't feel so bloody inadequate. My mother is being charged for something I know she didn't do. And here I am incapable of doing anything constructive to help." James held his head in despair unable to understand what was happening or even how it all came to this.

"Stop beating yourself up James, we will soon know the answers, Natalie has faith in this barrister who she knows, what is his name again Natalie?"

"Joseph M. Kaspian and he really is the best." Natalie smiled at David glad he was there to try and keep everything in perspective for James, who she knew was taking everything so hard. But who wouldn't? It was like a scene out of a bad movie gone wrong. There was absolutely no common ground for him to understand, nothing at all.

"Let's just wait until Joseph gets here. His flight arrives in approximately three hours and he is coming straight to the hotel to meet you James." Natalie said quietly, knowing they were miles away in their own minds and not really listening. "And Cathy and John will be here as well." She said.

Joseph stood there in the hotel room and his heart went out to the son of the woman he was defending and her family. He didn't understand much of what they were saying and though he hadn't met Maria yet, she did come across as a very strong woman. But this was her son, how could she hurt him like this? Surely he was owed some kind of explanation, but there was nothing.

"It doesn't matter how many people stand there swearing on oath, giving glowing reports on her good character. None of that will alter the fact that if she pleads guilty she will be sentenced accordingly."

"Is there nothing we can do?" James said, the anguish clearly in his voice

"If she is admitting to taking her father's life, then I'm afraid not. We are looking at a custodial sentence"

"John, is there nothing you can add?" Joseph said, looking directly at him. All eyes focused on John, all thinking the same.

"It is Maria's choice" he said with such sorrow it could be felt in the air around him.

"Yes, you are right, I shouldn't have asked. Maria holds the key to her own life and it is up to her to confirm what the truth is." said Joseph.

John appreciated the understanding, but he was still hurting inside. It was a terrible burden to carry around, but Maria had begged him, made him promise. The atmosphere in the room was overwhelming, it wasn't right, and he knew remaining quiet and keeping her secret wasn't going to make it any better. But he had no choice, he had given his word. And if Maria refused to say anything then that was her decision. John couldn't take any more; his head was hurting and the pressure was too much.

"I'm sorry" he said, his voice breaking. "I really am." And with that he turned and walked away.

The others watched silently as the door closed behind him, the air was filled with mixed feelings. Most were angry, they had wanted him, needed him to say something, anything. He was the only one who had been there with Maria.

"It's not up to John, it's up to Maria to tell the truth, only

245

she knows what really happened and she's chosen to remain quiet. It's too easy to blame John."

"You are right Mr.Kaspian" said Cathy quietly "but it still hurts."

"Please call me Joseph"

Cathy liked this man and felt a little better. "So what happens now Joseph" she said almost in a whisper.

"Tomorrow "he said "she will appear before the Magistrates court and they will then refer her to the Crown court because of the nature of the offence."

"Will she get bail?" she interrupted, horror stricken at the thought of Maria being locked up.

"She has a good chance" he smiled, hoping he looked more confident that he felt.

Maria did get bail and it was a further twelve months before her date came up for trial. During that period Joseph spent many long hours talking, asking questions, giving advice but it was to no avail. Maria refused to budge; her mind seemed to be set in stone. James went from being frustrated to annoyed to downright angry. He could not understand what or why, it was happening. Plus the fact his mother was doing absolutely nothing to help herself, didn't she care? he asked himself more than once. The whole family was experiencing extreme stress only Maria seemed to be in happy oblivion as she spent many an hour talking to her mother and enjoying her company. Ailsa was having more good days than ever, sometimes she seemed quite rational almost normal. The death of her husband never came into conversation. It was as if it never happened. She had never been so happy and this was what Maria had always wanted. To watch her smile, enjoy life, play with her grandchildren.

All too soon the date was upon them. She was going to court. As Joseph studied her, trying to understand, he was amazed at how composed she seemed to be. Her whole manner was unexpectedly calm. It was like it wasn't really happening, as if she was not involved in the fact that once she appeared before the judge and pleaded guilty, her whole life would change. And it would never, ever, be the same again.

She was going to be charged with murder, and everything inside him screamed of frustration and failure. He had tried, so very hard had he tried, but nothing he had said or done could convince her to change her mind.

"It doesn't have to be like this Maria" he said in one last attempt to get through to her.

"Yes, it does," she smiled, as the door opened and the two prison officers entered to escort her out into the courtroom.

No one spoke. Joseph thought he had failed and a great injustice was going to be done. But Maria was ready, she had made her decision. She had had moments of doubt, when she had wanted to scream and shout out loud that she didn't do it. "But then, would that have been the truth," she thought. If she was being truly honest, what her mother had done was only what she herself had subconsciously wanted to do all her life. So, did that make her any better than her mother? It might have been her mother's hand that took his life, but it was Maria herself who had wished it most.

She turned towards the window, her fingers felt the coldness of the bars as she gazed one last time out into the mountains in the distance. She smiled sadly.

"But what has been the price?" She asked herself feeling the tears hovering behind her eyes, questioning not what she had done, but had she done it right.

"Maria"

"She looked up into the eyes of the man she had come to love. The man who had tried so hard to make her plead 'not guilty', he looked at her beseechingly, his clear blue eyes almost begging her to reconsider. But she couldn't.

Joseph watched her intently, noticing the soft line of her lips, beautiful soft lips that no longer smiled, and he was angry. Never before had he felt so out of control.

"Why, was she pleading guilty?" He had learnt over the years, both in and out of court, to know when someone was telling the truth. Maria couldn't have murdered her own father, his whole being rejected it. No.....and yet, she had not uttered one word in her own defence. There was nothing she had helped him with. It was as if she wanted to go to prison.

Maria saw the changing expressions on his face, watched as his hand ran despairingly through his hair, and wanted to cry. She knew that after today there would be no more walking in the sunshine, feeling the wind upon her face or listening to his unending questions. Today her freedom would come to an end.

Reaching up she touched him gently on the face, his hand automatically reached out to hers. They stood silently looking into each other's eyes, the atmosphere charged with feelings that spoke volumes.

"Why? he asked.

As she went to walk through the doors, to hear the words that were to change her life forever, she turned.

"If I am being totally honest" she said quietly looking up at him. "I wanted that man dead, and that's what makes me guilty."

"Wanting some-one dead Maria is not the same as killing them, that's murder."

There was something about that last sentence that struck a chord in Maria's heart. It was the word killing, it became a reality. And the full impact of what she was doing came home to her. Her face paled.

"What is it?" he said with concern seeing her changing expression and sudden loss of colour.

"You are right," she whispered quietly. "I didn't kill him"

Joseph felt elated these were the very words he had tried for so long to get her to say.

"Then you are changing your plea, yes, to not guilty?"

"No" she said quietly.

"What do you mean then?"

"I don't know, I was responsible, believe me Joseph I was." She remembered how her mother had held her whispering 'I done it for you Maria, I done it for you.' And from that moment Maria did what she always did, she accepted responsibility.

Her face was like a mirror of many changing images. He watched her carefully and realised she would never believe in her own innocence. It was now up to him. Manslaughter, diminished responsibility, self-defence, the words were all there going round in his mind but for the first time, he felt his confidence bursting through his veins. This was no longer the end. It was the beginning.